A Hell of a Place to Die

Paul Bedford

A Black Horse Western

ROBERT HALE

ISBN 978-0-7198-2220-9

The Crowood Press
The Stable Block
Crowood Lane
Ramsbury
Marlborough
Wiltshire SN8 2HR

www.bhwesterns.com

Robert Hale is an imprint
of The Crowood Press

*For my three wonderful children – Oliver, Claudia and
Jonathan*

Typeset by
Derek Doyle & Associates, Shaw Heath
Printed and bound in Great Britain by
CPI Group (UK) Ltd, Croydon, CR0 4YY

A Hell of a Place to Die

Following on from *A Return to the Alamo,* Thomas Collins finds himself in Mexico with a detachment of Texas Rangers. Their mission is to escort the infamous dictator, Lopez de Santa Anna and his delectable daughter Ana de Luna inland from Veracruz, so that he can regain power and end the war with America. Collins soon realizes that far from assisting him, his men may well intend to slaughter Santa Anna in revenge for the Alamo siege a decade earlier. He is also accompanied by a young Robert E. Lee and the mysterious Francis Tylee, who in addition to possessing Samuel Colt's latest revolving repeating rifle appears to have his own murderous agenda. After leaving the coast, Collins and his disparate band fend off an attack by Mexican Cavalry, unintentionally destroy the cathedral in Xalapa whilst fighting the Irish Saint Patrick's Brigade and end up enduring a gruelling encounter at the prison fortress of Perote in the Mexican highlands.

By the same author

Blood On The Land
The Devil's Work
The Iron Horse
Pistolero
The Lawmen
The Outlaw Trail
Terror In Tombstone
The Deadly Shadow
Gone West
A Return To The Alamo
Taggart's Crossing

CHAPTER ONE

The one-ounce lead ball, measuring roughly seventy-one parts of one inch in diameter, slammed into the adobe wall behind which I was crouching. Cursing loudly I dropped flat and, not for the first time, wondered just what on earth I was doing there. Such thoughts were compounded by the fact that I had harboured bad feelings about the grubby little village the minute that I had clapped eyes on it. Under my appraising scrutiny it had appeared both too defensible and too quiet.

'Hey – Thomas, how's it feel having your own lead thrown at you, ha-ha-ha?'

Sergeant Kirby's feeble attempt at wit was direct and to the point as usual and, remarkably, he had used my given name rather than my now somewhat irrelevant rank. The fact that the Mexican Army was most definitely equipped with the out-dated (but quintessentially British) Brown Bess musket did little to improve my humour.

'Anyhow,' he continued remorselessly, 'before you get too attached to that dirt, what say we show these greasers who it is they're up against?'

I eased back one of the hammers of my shotgun, checked the copper percussion cap and then called back:

'When I discharge the first barrel, flank him.'

Under normal circumstances, announcing your plans within earshot of the enemy was almost guaranteed to ensure that you would hear God laugh. However, in this case it was highly unlikely that any ignorant Mexican conscript would comprehend the Queen's English, as spoken by an English gentleman.

'You'll have to take the house on your lonesome,' came the unhelpful reply. 'The sons of bitches are making off and we need screamers.'

The realization that I would have to offer myself up briefly as a target made my flesh crawl, but there was no other choice. At least I appeared to be up against smooth-bore muskets rather than the deadly accurate rifles favoured by my companions.

I drew in a deep breath and lurched to my feet. I thrust the 'two-shoot' gun over the wall and, hugging it tightly to my shoulder, swept it in a lateral arc. Off to my left, some thirty feet away, stood a small adobe hovel. It was from here that the shot had emanated. As I squinted against the harsh subtropical sunlight I made a most unwelcome discovery. Framed within the confines of the hovel's only visible window stood a solitary figure, resplendent in blue with scarlet facings.

'Regulars!'

Yet, directly faced with the gaping muzzles of my weapon, he reacted in the way least likely to save his own life. Swinging his musket into line, he frantically tried to focus on my position. Without hesitation I squeezed the first trigger. With a deafening roar the mixture of scrap metal and lead balls tore through the air. A fleck of copper scored my left cheek as though mocking my efforts, then I was back behind the protective wall.

Aware that my position was marked by the cloud of acrid smoke hanging in the air above me, I doubled over and ran awkwardly to my left. There was a deal of shouting around me, as my nearest comrades rushed forward, pursuing their own objectives. I cocked the second hammer, ran around the end of the dilapidated wall and made straight for the building. The window surround was scored with fresh indentations. Of the gaudily dressed infantryman there was no sign and yet, as shooting began around me, I could detect movement in the recesses of the room.

I charged headlong and poked the sawn-off barrels through the now vacant window space. I squeezed the second trigger. Again the piece roared in my hand, and this time it leapt back under the force of the unfettered recoil. Agonized screams came from within. I discarded the empty shotgun and drew my Paterson Colt revolver. I pulled back the hammer and hurled myself at the flimsy door. It collapsed under my weight and I found myself in a nightmare of smoke and shadow. As I struggled to adjust to the rapid change in light I became dimly aware of movement in front of me. Firing by instinct rather than aiming in the true sense, I swiftly discharged three of my five available chambers. In the enclosed space the din was overwhelming. I will never know what influence abruptly stilled my hand that day, but I was suddenly possessed by the absolute certainty that I was no longer under threat.

The sudden cessation of violent detonations left a strange stillness in the room which, of course, was pure illusion. Although I was vaguely aware of distant firing it was the eerie moaning and scuffling in other parts of the building that captured my attention. No longer assailed by summer sun or muzzle flashes, my eyes were adjusting to the gloom of the interior. What I saw filled me with sheer horror.

The blood-soaked creatures writhing before me were not battle-hardened Mexican regulars, but mere children, barely off their mothers' breasts.

By Christ! I thought, *I've attacked a house full of infants.*

7

Despite the intense summer heat a dreadful chill came over me as I scoured the room. Near the window lay the now nauseatingly disfigured 'soldier' in the blue-and-scarlet jacket. It appeared to be the only genuine item of military clothing that he possessed, which meant that he was either a deserter or, even worse, a mere civilian parading in ill-gotten finery before his family.

My revulsion turned to rage as I realized that he alone had brought down all this destruction on them. As the continued death agonies of his offspring filled my ears I kicked out savagely at his lifeless form.

'You stupid ignorant bastard!' I howled out. 'You brought all this on these children.'

Even as I unleashed the accusation I knew that I was deceiving myself. After all, I was the invader, and that knowledge only served to increase my anger. So incensed was I that I failed to register the movement behind me.

'You're a mite prickly, ain't you?'

With an animal snarl I raised my fully cocked revolver and swivelled round. Through the blood mist over my eyes I could just make out the heavily weathered features of the Texas Ranger, Sergeant Kirby. His calculating gaze took in my reaction immediately and he took a step back. Slowly he raised his empty right hand and spoke so softly that I barely heard him.

'Easy now, Thomas. You don't want to pop a cap on *me*.'

For long seconds I just stared at him, until at last the madness in my head subsided. I drew in a deep breath and eased the hammer down on a full chamber. Relief was evident on Kirby's visage as he watched the tension flow from me. The moaning in that charnel house had all but ceased and with it any chance of saving any life, so I sidestepped the ranger and walked out without a backward glance.

*

Ruefully, I wiped the sweat from my forehead and cast my gaze around the vast encampment, looking for a familiar face. Everywhere signs of the recent conflict were visible. Wounded men in various stages of distress were slumped on the hard ground. Blue-coated artillerymen were overhauling their pieces. Farriers were replacing lost or damaged horseshoes and the camp cooks were labouring to provide men with their first freshly cooked meal in days.

The siege of Monterrey in northern Mexico had been a gruelling and hard-fought struggle. My own traumatic encounter had taken place shortly afterwards, in a village between Monterrey and Saltillo, off to the south-west.

My roving glance fell on a long row of closely packed blankets, and suddenly my blood ran cold. There were roughly two-score bodies under those covers, and none of them had died in battle. Plague had arrived in the army, and that was another damn good reason for me to depart.

I jumped slightly as a familiar voice sounded off beside me.

'Every time I see an array like that, it makes me think on a slaver I once saw at the coast. Those blacks were packed tight, like spoons. 'Twas a fearful sight.'

Turning slightly, I regarded the rough-hewn visage of Sergeant Kirby.

'All the more reason for you to follow the lead of the "Goddamn British Empire" and outlaw slavery in your country,' I replied. 'It is a pernicious evil that brings credit to no man.'

Kirby's horny hand came down on my back in what I hoped was a comradely gesture.

'Pernicious is it? Hot damn! You'll run that mouth of yours off in the wrong company once too often. As it is, I come hotfoot to tell you the colonel is itching to jaw with you, and I ain't never worked for a colonel before. So haul your ass over there.'

*

Colonel John Coffee Hays, celebrated commander of the First Regiment, Texas Mounted, regarded me intently as I ducked my tall frame under his open-sided tent. Not for him the suffocating enclosure of his commanding general. He also managed without an honour guard at the entrance, but then, having witnessed his uncanny skill with Colt's revolvers, I knew that it would take an unusually reckless individual to accost him without good cause.

'Well now, Thomas, how goes it?'

'After seeing that row of festering blankets over yonder, I think that it's good fortune that we are all moving on.'

The colonel nodded gravely. 'The *vomito* rages fearfully. All the officers are under much apprehension over it.'

His eyes remained fixed on mine as he dropped easily into a folding canvas chair.

'Set you down.'

Having known him for over two years I could tell that he had much to impart, so I willingly complied. Anything that that man had to say was worthy of my full attention. Similar in age to myself, small and slight of stature, he led his volunteer rangers by sheer force of personality. His abilities on the frontier were unequalled, and he alone had developed the tactics for combating the Comanche menace that so blighted the land. In his strangely high voice he now proceeded to describe exactly what was expected of me.

'You have been appointed a major in the Texas Mounted. You will command the ranger escort that accompanies that butcher Santa Anna back into Mexico. Our government, in its wisdom, has done a deal with him to make peace with the United States once he regains power.'

No Texan could ever forget the rout that the Mexican general had brought about at the Alamo. Despite my stunned

10

surprise at this amazing news, that was the thought upper-most in my mind.

'Surely Texas Rangers are the last people who should be accompanying him?'

'True, true. Yet they are also the finest irregular cavalry that the United States possesses and are ideally suited to this task. That's why you, as an Englishman of proven grit, have command. You are the least likely to harbour any hatred towards him.'

Recognizing my disquiet, my interlocutor abruptly changed tack, and now it was my turn to witness unease in his expression.

'Let me ask you something else, Thomas. We are all of us to travel down the Gulf of Mexico to Veracruz by paddle frigate. Have you ever travelled on one of those steam con-traptions – other than the one you sank, of course, ha-ha?'

There was something in his forced laughter that occa-sioned me to stare long and hard at him. I had just witnessed something that I had never thought to see. The renowned Indian-fighter was actually nervous at the prospect of a sea voyage. I smiled at him reassuringly.

'Don't concern yourself, Jack,' I replied, 'they are perfectly safe. I travelled all the way across the Atlantic in one, and I'm here to tell the tale.'

'Only I don't swim so well,' he replied, looking a little sheepish.

'Oh, that's of no account,' I told him, maintaining a casual air. 'It wouldn't save you if you could. If you did happen to fall overboard the odds are that you'd be swept up into the huge side paddles, knocked senseless and crushed to a sickening bloody pulp before you even had a chance to drown.'

As his eyes widened in horror I leaned forward, patted his arm.

'But then they do say that there's always worse trouble at

sea,' I added with a chuckle.

The light began to dawn in his sharp mind and I scurried from his tent, my own laughter ringing in my ears.

CHAPTER TWO

'Defend yourselves!'

I had only just stepped out of the USS *Mississippi*'s gig on to the beach at Veracruz, so such a cry was the last thing that I wished to hear. Yet the tone of the distant but somehow familiar voice left no doubt about the situation.

Even in the gathering gloom a glance over at the city walls was enough confirmation. A large skirmishing party was issuing from a sally port directly facing us, some two hundred yards away. As they spread out, muskets at the ready, I bellowed at Lieutenant Tylee, the naval officer in command of our frail craft.

'We need a barricade. Get your men to drag that boat on to the beach.'

I unslung the sawn-off shotgun from behind my back and removed the length of canvas that I had wrapped around it as protection from the waves. I retracted both hammers and swiftly checked the seating of the copper percussion caps.

His Excellency, the extravagantly named Antonio de Padua Maria Severino Lopez de Santa Anna y Perez de Lebron, soon to be my constant companion, demonstrated his own particular grasp of soldiering by ignoring everyone else and dropping flat on the beach. In his right hand was a deadly but temperamental six-barrelled pepper-box revolver.

I twisted round and yelled at his two attendants to drop down behind the now upturned boat. Without waiting to see if they complied I threw myself on to the pebbles, next to the man whom I was supposed to protect at all costs.

The safest place for any soldier in almost all circumstances is either flat on the ground or dug in below it. As if to emphasize this, a pebble leapt into the air only inches from my face. From around us and before us, firing broke out as the Mexican skirmishers drew closer. On either side of us we had a mixture of blue-clad regulars from the invasion force and volunteers outfitted to personal choice in buckskins and slouch hats. My own group of new arrivals, deliberately separated from the rank-and-file rangers, was somewhat isolated, yet they appeared to be attracting the majority of the enemy force. But to what purpose? Were the Mexicans seeking to take hostages or merely to slaughter us as an act of war?

The only saving grace was that they were afoot; otherwise we would have been swiftly overrun. The nearest group, numbering some two dozen, was by now about one hundred yards away: extreme range for a Brown Bess musket but not for Lieutenant Tylee's remarkable Colt repeating rifle. He dropped down to my right, took careful aim, held his breath and squeezed the trigger. There was a sharp crack as the ball left the rifled barrel and went spinning off up the beach.

The Mexican was in mid-stride as it caught him in the gut. With a shriek he doubled over and collapsed to the ground. A very painful and most likely prolonged death awaited him. One down, but many remained.

'Are your men armed?' I asked Tylee urgently.

'Belt knives only. They were not intended to be a shore party.'

'Then we must make do,' I declared grimly. 'How many more balls does that thing hold, Lieutenant?'

'Six, and one empty chamber,' he replied before adding

wryly, 'In expectation of a rough crossing.'

Knowing that we might well face an opposed landing, I had dispensed with such precautions. I smiled encouragingly.

'Well then, you'd better make them all count,' I commented.

Finding little resistance from our section of the beach the skirmishers abandoned all caution and came at the run. I tucked the shotgun butt tightly into my shoulder, resisted all natural instincts and held my fire. From beside me there was a loud report as Tylee fired again.

At fifty yards some of our assailants discharged their muskets at the upturned boat, but still I held firm.

Forty yards passed, as did thirty. Another bang sounded from the repeating rifle and I caught a whiff of sulphur. At twenty yards I squeezed the first trigger. With a comforting roar the piece expelled its deadly load. To the sound of agonized screams I pivoted some twenty degrees and discharged the second barrel. Again the fierce recoil pounded my shoulder and I blinked involuntarily as a fleck of copper scored my eye.

The tempestuous wind that had been lashing our ship for days past swiftly dispelled all the powder smoke. That and the relentless naval bombardment allowed me to view the carnage with a clarity rarely available in night actions. Three of our immediate assailants were down, wailing in their own private hell. The remainder hesitated momentarily, then someone bellowed out:

'*Pinche date prisa!*'

A seventeen-inch socket bayonet, projecting from a forty-two-inch musket barrel, is a fearsome weapon at close range. Several of these were now advancing on our position. The urge to flee was almost overwhelming, tempered only by the knowledge that I had the storm-tossed Gulf at my back.

With an oath I leapt to my feet and hurled the empty

15

shotgun at the advancing soldiers. Tylee's rifle cracked yet again, which helped to steady me. I grabbed my revolver and thumbed back the hammer, thereby releasing the retractable trigger. Stubbornly standing my ground, I aimed beyond the nearest steel point and fired. A scream testified to my accuracy but I had no time to observe the fall of shot. Three more times I went through the same process: cock, aim and fire. The last ball entered a skirmisher through his left cheek and deflected off a set of rotten teeth before taking the side of his head off. As blood and brain matter sprayed over his nearest companion the tide of battle turned. Although still outnumbering us, the Mexican *soldados* began to waver.

In my peripheral vision I became aware that Santa Anna had clambered to his feet and was now standing next to me. But to what purpose? Surely he would not enter the fray against his own countrymen. With just the one chamber remaining, I pointed my weapon at a short stocky fellow directly before me. He alone seemed intent on pressing forward with their faltering attack.

As that luckless warrior observed the muzzle of my Colt line up on his torso he froze. A mixture of terror and indecision registered on his swarthy features. His musket must have been empty, for he made no attempt to shoot me with it. Yet he did not turn and run. With certain death looming, a wild look bordering on madness entered his eyes and I squeezed the trigger for the final time.

There was an ominous pop and then nothing. *Hangfire!*

As a torrent of urine splashed over his worn boots a look of almost indescribable relief lit up his face. That swiftly changed to one of ferocious hatred as he realized what I had just done. He swung up his musket and positioned himself to lunge at me. Moonlight glinted on the vicious wrought-iron bayonet, now merely inches from my face. Out of ammunition, with no room to manoeuvre, I was completely helpless.

16

Off to my left Santa Anna released the cord around his neck and shrugged off the voluminous cloak. Even in the indifferent light, there was no mistaking the full-dress uniform of which he was so proud. Its effect on the lowly foot soldier was profound. Total confusion was now evident as he turned to face the regal apparition. In so doing he unwittingly allowed the deadly bayonet to lurk in the vicinity of Santa Anna's throat. The conscript's natural subservience to authority then asserted itself and he hurriedly lowered the weapon. Finding his voice he stammered: '*Perdon, mi General.*'

Santa Anna nodded his acknowledgement, then coolly raised his pepperbox, and squeezed the trigger. With an unexpected crash all six barrels discharged simultaneously. *Chainfire!*

The lethal array of .31-calibre lead balls caught the soldier full in the face and blew him off his feet. The unanticipated recoil rocked Santa Anna back on his heels and with a curse he flung the temperamental revolving pistol to the ground. One glance at his victim was enough for my stomach. The point-blank volley and the muzzle flash had reduced his face to smouldering wreckage.

From off to my left came heavy rapid firing of a kind that I had not heard before. It could only have come from men armed with revolvers, yet the tone was altogether deeper than that of my Paterson Colt. Whatever the source, it was sufficient to send the remaining skirmishers scurrying back to the city walls.

Not all made it however. One of Tylee's oarsmen, emboldened by our successful defence, leapt forward with the speed of a cat. Overhauling a fleeing soldier, he sank his knife into the back of the man's neck. With an agonized wail the Mexican threw his arms out wide as though in supplication, then fell forward on to the beach. With murderous glee the sailor struck again and again, until a sharp command from his

17

officer brought him to his senses.

'Belay there, Shadrach! He's deader than Davy Crockett.'

Santa Anna, who had recovered his equilibrium, flushed red with anger at the calculated remark, but wisely held his tongue. He well knew that he was not among friends.

With the field of battle cleared, the other sailors advanced and quite blatantly began rifling the pockets of the fallen. After regarding the scavengers with distaste for some moments I glanced over at Tylee who, short sword in hand, stood surveying the carnage. Returning my enquiring stare, he merely shrugged. If he had intended to make a comment it would have been lost anyway, overwhelmed by an ear-splitting shriek from the seashore. I spun round, to see a distraught Ana de Luna, Santa Anna's female companion, pointing down behind the upturned longboat. It could only have been their secretary, Señor Canalizo, and so it proved.

A .71-calibre musket ball had punched through his forehead, and had presumably removed the back of his skull. He lay flat on his back, surrounded by blood and matter, victim to a very unfortunate chance shot by one of his own countrymen. This was a singularly bad start and I said as much to his erstwhile employer.

His Excellency appeared to be more troubled by the effect of the unstable terrain on his cork leg than by the abrupt demise of his employee. At our first meeting on board ship he had appeared both tall and regal, albeit with a fleshy, decadent face. Now however he was sweating heavily in his thick clothing and appeared infirm and vulnerable. He limped over to join me and hurriedly gestured a sign of the cross before moving on to take Ana in his arms. His expression betrayed genuine concern and affection as he murmured tenderly to her in his own language.

His travelling companion was quite obviously his much younger and extremely beautiful lover. So much for the story of his delivering her to her husband in Mexico City. Then again, I supposed that that much could be true and that he was merely pleasuring himself in the meantime.

My cynical musings were brusquely interrupted by a familiar voice.

'What is it with you? Every time I see you, you're surrounded by dead bodies.'

I twisted round and regarded my friend Sergeant Kirby with unashamed joy. Of medium height and stocky build, he was older than the average ranger. With buckskin trousers and a hairy visage, he looked the archetypal frontiersman. As we had travelled on separate ships it was marvellous to see his friendly face. Not that he looked any too friendly at that particular moment. As his gaze took in the gloriously attired figure of Santa Anna he snapped off a question.

'Who the hell's that pus weasel?'

I knew full well whom he meant, but for the life of me could not think of a suitable reply.

The ranger persisted.

'He your prisoner or what?'

'Something like that,' I mumbled, anxious to move on. Still pointing my revolver at the ground, I mentioned my recent mishap.

'They will do that,' he answered non-committedly, hard eyes still fixed on the general.

I could tell that he knew I was hedging and that he didn't like it one bit. So I tried again. I simply could not miss the oversized revolver in Kirby's grasp. It was truly enormous.

'What is *that*?'

At last he looked back at me and his expression softened somewhat.

'This, my friend, is a Colt Walker. Cap'n Walker wanted a belt gun that would bring down a Comanche devil – or his horse. He and Samuel Colt came up with this cannon.'

I placed my own suddenly diminutive weapon on the pebbles, reached over and accepted the proffered gun. God's blood, it was heavy! It was well over one foot long, with six chambers available; I could not imagine slipping a brace of those into any belt of mine.

Kirby smiled as he watched me appraise the revolver.

'That's a .44-calibre with a sixty-grain charge. It'll stop anything it hits.'

In spite of its daunting weight I was quite sold on the concept.

'Where can I obtain a couple of these, Sergeant Kirby? I'll require a horse to carry them, mind. As befits my status as an officer.'

Winking broadly, I handed back the Colt Walker and then looked around me. Ostensibly I was surveying the general scene, but more particularly I was earnestly hoping that Santa Anna might have had the good sense to slip on his cloak. I was most gratified to observe that he had done so, because until Colonel Hays informed his men of the true situation his safety could not be assured.

Turned back to the grizzled ranger.

'There is much that I would discuss with you, but first I must report to the colonel,' I stated. 'Where might I find him?'

Kirby told me, then looked quizzically over at the two cloaked figures.

'And I suppose they're going too, huh?'

'Most indubitably, old chap,' I replied, affecting the air of an English aristocrat. My friend shook his head sadly.

'I've been lettered since I was twelve, but I still ain't got a goddamn clue what you done said,' he remarked. 'I just hope you know what you're doing, is all.'

'Only sometimes,' I responded drily. With that I turned and walked over to where the two Mexicans lingered. The general was obviously working hard to curb his impatience. It did not suit his temperament to be kept waiting by one so junior in rank as myself, but then his was a unique situation. He was currently confronted with an American invasion of his own nation, during which he had just murdered one of his own men, a fact that seemed to trouble him not one iota. But he was sensitive to the dangers lurking amongst the Texan Irregulars. They, of all people, had good reason to want him dead, and they had little respect for authority.

As a matter of form I announced to the general and his companion my intention of reporting to Colonel Hays, adding that for their own safety they would do well to accompany me. The general scrutinized me for some moments before nodding his assent.

'*Gracias*, Major Collins. I must congratulate you on your fighting prowess. Your ferocious defence saved us from sharing Canalizo's fate, and I now find myself in your debt.'

I bowed from the waist by way of acknowledgement before answering:

'That gentleman must be a grievous loss to you. To die under such circumstances was such a waste. Yet you did not hesitate to destroy your own countryman, even though he was no threat to you.'

Santa Anna smiled sardonically at me, looking every inch the proud dictator.

'You must understand one thing, *por favor*. That *soldado*, he make a very grave mistake. He allow his weapon to threaten me. Me, his general, his president, his saviour!'

It occurred to me that at that moment he was none of those things and, in all fairness, the delectable Ana, with her jet-black hair and voluptuous figure, looked vaguely uncomfortable. Her lover, however, was in full flow and seemingly unaffected by the fact that we were standing on an exposed beach, at night, under naval bombardment, surrounded by numerous cadavers.

He was eventually silenced in the best of all possible ways.

'Mister, I ain't decided just who you are yet, but I'm getting powerful tired listening to you lead the hosannas.'

Santa Anna stared at Kirby in stunned amazement. It was clear that he had not comprehended all that had been said.

Placing myself directly between Kirby and the general, I stared unblinkingly at the sergeant.

'These two people are in my charge. If you insist on provoking an incident on this godforsaken beach Colonel Jack himself may well have to shoot you.'

Then, in an attempt to lighten the mood, I continued with a colloquial term that I had overheard on occasion. 'Are you backed up yet?'

The slightest hint of a smile showed on Kirby's features as he replied. 'Some.'

'In that case we will take our leave.' With a courteous sweep of my hand, I gestured for the two Mexicans to depart. As I moved off I added by way of consolation: 'I promise to give you a full explanation when I am able.'

The three of us stumbled along the beach and I could almost feel Kirby's eyes burning into my back. When he and the other rangers found out just who was in my charge there could well be hell to pay.

It soon became apparent that the invasion had progressed beyond that of a mere beachhead. I began to sense that the whole city was encircled. Why else would the defenders even attempt to mount sorties from the seaward side, in full view of the American fleet, unless they were unable to sweep round from the rear?

As we made our slow progress over the pebbles we past through groups of men ranged about on the shore. At last, and with great relief, we made it off the beach and on to firm ground. I knew that if the rangers were present their commanding officer could not be far away. So it proved. Colonel John Coffee Hays was to be found bivouacked behind a clutch of huge boulders, most certainly proof against musket balls and even solid shot. As we approached a ranger pointed one of the huge new revolvers menacingly in our direction. Then, recognizing me, he pulled back to allow our approach. Crouched over a small fire, Hays looked up. His keen glance took in both myself and my two companions. Swiftly he rose to greet me.

'I am gratified to see you in rude health, Thomas, but I was expecting Major Collins and *three* travellers. I hope you didn't misplace one on the crossing.'

Hays's mind was obviously as sharp and alert as ever, but something in his face disturbed me. There was greyness to his pallor and he had a haggard look about him that I had not noticed on any of our previous encounters.

'You appear somewhat reduced, Jack. Please God it is not the fever. And yes, Secretary Canalizo met an unfortunate end at the hands of his own countrymen.'

'Do not trouble yourself over me, Thomas, it is nothing as life-threatening as the fever. I am plagued by toothache. I believe I must shortly place myself in Travis's tender clutches.' Wincing, he added, 'He is reputedly adept at removing rotten molars with blacksmith's tools. I don't mind telling you, I'd rather face a Comanche Buck who was after my scalp!'

His eyes flitted over to the two 'travellers' and then back to me. In a hushed tone he continued:

'That particular death was a little hard on the hired help; there's many hereabouts as would welcome Santa Anna's demise. Anyhow, I suppose you'd better make the introductions, but keep the son of a bitch covered up.'

I had not known what to expect in a meeting between the Texas Ranger leader and a man who, even now, could not

23

accept the loss of that province. Not for the first time on that side of the Atlantic I received a surprise. I stood aside as I watched the colonel approach them. The seemingly permanent naval bombardment provided a fitting background for the occasion. The stage was lit by bursts of brilliant light from the varied ordnance.

Hays removed his hat and bowed graciously before the two cloaked figures. Santa Anna responded somewhat less enthusiastically, whilst in contrast Ana drew back her hood and favoured him with a devastating smile. I chuckled to myself. Even the normally unflappable ranger showed signs of having been caught off guard. But then what man wouldn't be? She was absolutely gorgeous!

Hays's eyes lingered on her features for long seconds before he managed to collect his thoughts.

'I am enchanted to meet you, *señora*. I had of course been warned of your arrival, but nothing had prepared me for your beauty.' He smiled before giving a gentle sigh. 'And so I implore you, please do not take offence from what I am about to say to His Excellency.'

The general assumed a wary expression and I could feel the tension suddenly build within me. Relatively short in stature, Hays had to look up as he addressed the Mexican, but there was no doubting his command of the situation.

'General, I am instructed by General Scott to provide you with an escort under the command of Major Collins here. I am informed that on your return to Mexico City you will endeavour to bring about a cessation of hostilities. I do not know what you have been offered to bring this about, nor do I care.'

The insult was there for all to witness, but the colonel gave Santa Anna no time to react.

'But I am expected to place a number of my men in danger to achieve this,' he continued. 'So if you live up to your reputation and play us false, then I will personally hunt you down and send you to perdition. You have my oath on that.'

Hays paused to let his words sink in. Santa Anna had remained inscrutable throughout, but I felt sure that he had understood the magnitude of the threat. A small nerve was working under his right eye and he refrained from offering any bluster in return. It occurred to me that he might well have heard of the ranger's lethal exploits against the Comanches. After all, until the American invasion they had been Northern Mexico's most implacable foe.

'You will now excuse me while I confer with Major Collins. My man here will show you where to rest – safe, one would hope, from your own guns.' Bowing slightly to Ana he remarked, 'Your servant, *señora*.' Then he turned away.

The interview was over; it occurred to me that neither of the two Mexicans had been given the slightest chance to respond. The designated ranger led his charges away, and we were alone.

'Ha! I'll wager he remembers that conversation,' I burst out.

'It is right that he should,' replied the colonel bleakly. 'I meant every word. But now, on to other matters.'

I dropped gratefully to the ground, where I sat and listened as he proceeded to tell me of the true situation in and around Veracruz. As I thought, the walled city had been completely surrounded but was being stoutly defended by Brigadier General Juan Morales and some four thousand troops. That resourceful officer had refused to treat with the invading army. Until Scott was able to land his heavy siege guns it would thus remain in Mexican hands and he could not do that whilst the storm persisted. The ownership of the city did not directly affect my party, as we were to be heading inland. But it did mean that we would be behind enemy lines from the moment that we set off. To his credit, Hays did not attempt to instil any false hopes.

'My understanding is that the hinterland and beyond is in chaos. Some may welcome you as their saviour from a despotic regime, whilst others may see you as a foreign devil, solely intent on rape and plunder.'

'The latter prospect sounds more attractive to me,' I responded, desperately attempting to inject a little levity. The ranger's expression, influenced by the twin evils of responsibility and toothache, remained gloomy as he continued:

'That's not the half of it. You also have Santa Anna's reputation to contend with. Will he be received with open arms or musket balls?'

Before I could comment the sounds of angry voices rose above the clamour of naval gunfire. Foremost among them was Sergeant Kirby's. We got to our feet and as we stepped out into the open I heard him very clearly.

'It come to me now! You be that tarnel cocksucker, what burnt all our boys in San Antonio!'

Directly before us stood Santa Anna, stripped of his voluminous cloak and therefore visible in all his bemedalled glory. Kirby had forced him up against a boulder and was probing his throat with a wicked-looking knife. Fresh blood glistened in the moonlight and it was obvious to all that the general was about to die. Standing close by, Ana was wringing her hands.

'*Madre de Dios!*' she screamed out.

Ignoring her theatrics, Hays pointed his Paterson Colt directly at the ranger and eased back the hammer.

'Sergeant Kirby!'

The familiar and unmistakable authority in his voice somehow penetrated the other man's bloodlust and he froze like a statue.

The ranger leader then issued a stark warning, uncannily echoing my own earlier one.

'I count you as a true friend and would trust you with my

life, but if you do not lower that blade I will surely parole you to Jesus.'

The sergeant turned as though in a trance, then blinked twice in rapid succession. He took in Hays's belligerent stance, then glanced over at me. Only then did he slowly lower his weapon. As the immediate threat subsided Santa Anna showed some of the fire that had to be present in a man such as he. Although undoubtedly shaken, he levered himself off the boulder and launched a torrent of invective at his assailant.

'*Bastardo! Pinche gringo cerdo!*'

The rest was too rapid for me to even distinguish, but his meaning was clear for all to hear and required no translation. Kirby swung back to face him, knife at the ready.

'You prancing peacock! I'll gut you like a fish.'

My heart leapt as a shot rang out next to me. A .36-calibre ball punched into the earth at the ranger's feet. I caught a whiff of sulphur as the strong wind swept the black powder smoke past me.

'So long as you remain under my command, Sergeant Kirby, you will obey my orders.' As the colonel spoke he again cocked his revolver. 'Clear?'

Kirby backed away from the object of his anger, then reluctantly sheathed his blade. He seemed anything but cowed, but a discipline of sorts appeared to have been reasserted.

'I reckon so,' he replied gruffly.

'Good,' commented Hays, He eased the hammer down and replaced the revolver in his belt. By now a sizeable audience of curious rangers had gathered round and he took advantage of this to state his case.

'Before you stands, in all his splendour, General Lopez de Santa Anna,' he said in a loud but high voice. 'All of you will know him for what he is.'

This information was greeted with disbelief, followed by

growls of anger. But, mindful of what they had just witnessed, they all listened as their leader continued:

'He has been placed in my care by General Scott, who does not have to explain his reasons for this to you. When he travels inland some of you will form his escort under Major Collins. Under the circumstances you fellows may seem to be a strange choice, but you are without doubt the finest men for the task. Whatever your personal feelings you will treat the general with courtesy and above all ensure his safety.'

Colonel Hays paused to allow all this to sink in. His gaze swept over all those present as he continued:

'All of you men know me well. Believe me when I say that this mission is of vital importance to the outcome of the war. Any ranger who disobeys the major will answer to me. Tell your compadres what you saw and heard here and don't go misremembering.'

As if by celestial intervention the end of his speech was brought to a rousing conclusion by a burst of gunfire from the city walls. Our growing numbers had attracted unwelcome attention, and lead balls began to pepper the ground around us.

'Scatter,' yelled Kirby. 'Those boys are shooters.'

With his words ringing in everyone's ears, the gathering rapidly dispersed.

It was some time later when my visitor arrived. I had attempted to get some sleep, but the thunderous din had prevented that. Just as he materialized before me all the ships' guns became still. No impresario could have staged it better. Total silence settled like a blanket. It really was most disconcerting, but as he moved closer I was able to make out the blue woollen uniform, with the embroidered bars on the shoulder strap.

'My name is Lee, Major Collins: Robert Lee. I am a captain

of engineers, currently attached to General Scott's staff.'

I to my feet and accepted his proffered hand. The steady moonlight allowed me a good view of him. Of medium height and build, he possessed a full head of dark wavy hair and a luxurious moustache.

As we regarded each other with mutual interest I was struck by the calm certainty in his eyes, which enhanced his reassuringly competent air. Favouring him with a warm smile I replied:

'I am most impressed with your entrance.'

His quiet laugh seemed to complement his pronounced Southern accent.

'You seek to endow me with the abilities of a wizard. Alas, my timing was pure chance. They are merely resting the crews, and allowing the guns to cool.'

Motioning for him to sit, I dropped to my haunches opposite him.

'What brings a captain of engineers into our midst, I wonder?'

Lee drew in a deep breath, as though preparing to deliver a speech.

'I am here to provide whatever assistance I can to you and your men. Be assured that I am fully aware of your mission, and the tortuous complexities that you face. Although Santa Anna knows this land intimately you do not, which is not an ideal situation.

'One of my duties for "Old Fuss and Feathers" has been to carry out a reconnaissance of the surrounding countryside and, more especially, of the various routes to Mexico City. The capital is some two hundred and fifty miles from here and seven thousand feet above sea level. Scott's next objective is Xalapa, some fifty-five miles from here, on one of the two main highways to Mexico City.

'He cannot set off without first capturing this port. It is

vital to his line of supply. Unfortunately, you can't wait around for him to do that. You have a possible future president to deliver. The sooner peace breaks out, the sooner we can all go home alive.

'Therefore, I am instructed to accompany your party, as a scout if you will. But only as far as Xalapa. That's as far as I have reconnoitred and I will be of no use to you beyond there.'

'I'll be very grateful to have you along,' I replied whole-heartedly. Even on such short acquaintance there was something about Robert Lee that inspired confidence and that quality influenced my next remark.

'The particular complexities of this mission mean that it is very hard for me to know whom to trust – and that includes my old friends in the Texas Rangers.'

As I revealed my concerns I became aware that Lee's glance was drifting off to one side.

Following his line of sight, I observed Lieutenant Tylee scrutinizing us, the frown on his face very evident. I could only assume that he had overheard our conversation; the thought stoked the fires of anger that always seemed to smoulder within me. Rising up to my full height I called out to him.

'I can't abide skulkers, Mr Tylee.'

His reply was not in the least conciliatory.

'If I am to be excluded from all discourse over our mission, then I am left with little choice.'

'Your continued role in my mission is a source of puzzle-ment to me,' I threw back. 'You delivered us safely to the beach and aided our defence of it. For that I am grateful, but I fail to see what more you have to offer. Our journey takes us inland, far beyond the range of your Paixhans guns.'

'I can ride and I can shoot – and you overlook one thing: I am here at the express request of the commanding general, so you have little choice in the matter.'

He had me there and he knew it. But why was it so damned important for him to accompany us? Whatever the reason, I seemed to be stuck with the bugger and if I had to be burdened with him I might as well utilize him.

'Very well then, Mr Tylee. You will oblige me by reporting to Colonel Hays immediately. You will request mounts for both of us, as well as a brace apiece of Mr Colt's newest revolver. Also, you will ensure that horses have been provided for the general and his – er – companion. When you have accomplished that I suggest you get some sleep.'

The lieutenant accepted all this without demur. After executing a formal salute he turned and strode off. Lee followed, leaving me with nothing to do but sleep. I had a feeling that that would be a commodity in short supply over the following few days.

CHAPTER THREE

'*Buenos dias*, Major Collins.'

Morning had arrived in the blink of an eye and those words, smoothly uttered, announced that my two charges were up and about. I groaned inwardly. I had slept soundly, but not for anywhere near long enough, and had been hoping for some time alone in which to collect my thoughts. But it was not to be.

'Well, ain't he the one!'

That comment, reeking of sarcasm, emanated from an unidentified ranger, and served as a warning of what awaited me.

With the coming of full daylight Santa Anna had discarded his heavy boat cloak; this unfortunately had had the effect of announcing his presence to the world. My own experiencing of our first day ashore under a tropical sun prompted some sympathy for the man, but not enough to allay my concern.

'You do not aid our cause by displaying that uniform, General,' I remarked.

The man drew in his stomach, inflated his chest, and proceeded to display some of the fire that had no doubt driven him to the dizzy heights of power.

'*No entiendo, señor.* This is *my* country, *sí*? How am I to draw my people to me if they cannot see me?'

'I realize that,' I countered, 'but my understanding is that not everyone will welcome your return.'

'It is your task to protect me from any such lost souls, is it not?'

Santa Anna had an annoying habit of turning statements into questions. There could be no doubt that he was as much a politician as a soldier, nor that our exchange was achieving little, other than to delay the expedition's departure.

I glanced over at the far more edifying sight of Señora de Luna. By the light of day she looked good enough to eat. Her almost skin-tight outfit, smooth golden complexion and lustrous black hair combined to such effect that I positively ached with desire for her.

I excused myself and strode off to take my first good look at the hinterland in daylight. The area immediately around the city walls and along the coast was a distinctly unappealing arid expanse, broken by numerous high sand dunes. Beyond the city and the immediate coastal area was a range of hills leading off into the interior. Once up there we would be clear of any threat from the city. But we would also be on our own, beyond any support from the American forces.

Colonel Hays had left it for me to work out the details of our departure. After some deliberation I determined that we should lead our horses on foot until we were well away from the city walls. That would reduce the likelihood of our being seen and pursued. The Mexican commander was energetically launching frequent forays against our soldiers and I did not wish for us to provoke any such incident. Yet what one hopes for and what one gets can often be separated by a cold hole in the ground.

The US forces had constructed hastily built breastworks around the city walls, fortified by small arms and light artillery. I now assembled my own party behind one of these

33

installations. In total we numbered twenty souls. In addition to the two Mexicans and myself, there were Lee, Tylee, Sergeant Kirby and fourteen Texas Rangers. They were all volunteers, assigned to me by the colonel. Since they all now knew the identity of the man that they were to protect I did just wonder if any of them had an ulterior motive for coming along. Yet I recognized that the mission would have far less chance of success if we used regular US troops. The Texas Ranger force contained some of the finest horsemen, scouts and offensive fighters on the continent.

They were also rough and ready frontiersmen, used to living on the edge of civilization and, like most young men, they were full of lust and passion. I had noticed the way that some of them were regarding Ana. Their eyes were hungry, and their scarcely concealed gestures were obscene. If she was aware of this she gave no sign, but for me it was one more problem amongst many.

Two of the rangers I knew well. I had served with Travis and Davey Jackson before. Some of the others I knew by sight, but had no knowledge of their character. Still, I would just have to work with what I had been given.

To his credit, Tylee had done exactly as instructed. Everybody appeared to be well mounted and I noticed that my own horse had two saddle holsters containing the new revolvers.

As I surveyed my small detachment Sergeant Kirby approached, sporting a decidedly grim demeanour. It was plain to see what he thought of our assignment. He might be a volunteer, but he didn't have to like it. Before he had time to speak I took him by the arm and led him away from the others.

'Listen, I need to know that I have your support,' I whispered to him urgently. 'Forget the other officers. Lee is only with us to Xalapa and I don't trust Tylee. General Scott has pressed him on me for no apparent reason. You are effectively my second in command. The others look up to you and I can't do this without you.'

That was a hell of an admission for any commanding officer and he knew it. After staring at me long and hard, he finally gave an exaggerated shrug of his shoulders.

'What the hell! I guess anything's better than waiting around this burgh for the bloody flux or the goddamned plague to hit us.'

I was on the point of rejoining the main group, but the ranger had more to say.

'Well, you've got your new horse pistols and that's good. But if you have to bring down any of them droop-eyed sons of bitches think on this: the spring on the loading rammer can't handle the recoil. Odds on it'll drop down after firing and lock up the cylinder. So just you grab the arm and snap it back on up.'

He winked at me and turned away to rejoin his rangers, then called back over his shoulder, 'Thought you should know, you being our officer and all.'

It was time to depart, but two people were missing. I had expected that Jack Hays would see us off, but he was not there and, coincidentally, Ranger Travis was also absent. Then it came to me. The rotten tooth!

Cursing their timing, I decided to move out regardless. I called down the length of the dismounted column to Davey Jackson. When I first met him he had been young and inexperienced, with a misplaced loathing of redcoats. Thankfully all that had changed and he was now a seasoned campaigner whom I could rely on.

'You will present my apologies to Colonel Hays, but we can't wait. You will offer him much joy on his new, hopefully pain-free gap in his teeth. When Travis has finished his doctoring, you will bring him on at the double.'

With an abrupt 'Yo,' Davey moved off.

'Move them out, Sergeant,' I ordered, and I set off at a brisk pace.

In reality our pace would be governed by the slowest member of the column; namely Santa Anna. With only one good leg and an obvious penchant for good living, he was not ideally suited to vigorous progress.

In single file we eighteen individuals led our horses towards the south-west. I intended to maintain that heading until we were out of sight of the city, then veer west-north-west for the remainder of the journey to Xalapa. As we moved away from both the fortifications and the gulf, we weaved our way through the sand dunes. Observing that the general was already making hard going of it, I came to a rapid decision.

'This subterfuge is pointless,' I called back. 'Mount up.'

I hauled myself into the unfamiliar saddle and quickly checked the fastenings of the holsters. It was some weeks since I had ridden anywhere, and it felt strange to have horse-flesh between my thighs again. Observing the others, I noticed that Ana, in her provocatively tight outfit, was riding instinctively and with natural grace. Likewise Santa Anna, once mounted, was transformed. He carried himself with regal aplomb, as though at the head of a conquering army. All the rangers had been born in a saddle, so naturally their skill was effortless.

A fusillade of shots rang out behind us and I looked back towards the city. The Mexican commander had sent a group of skirmishers on foot straight for the American lines, so that the defenders had had to concentrate to rebuff them. This action had allowed some three-score cavalry to cut through unhindered. They were now in hot pursuit and we had very little time. Our own horses were not up to a prolonged chase. Until recently they had been aboard ship in the most frightful conditions. Kirby voiced my exact thoughts.

'They're coming full chisel, and these horses ain't got the wind, Thomas.'

'I know,' I bellowed back. 'We'll have to stand them off.'

Captain Lee pulled up level with me.

'Sir, I believe that rise over yonder will serve. Let us ride these beasts as though we have just stolen them.'

Following his gaze I noticed that, some distance off to our right, the ground rose to form a small knoll. Jabbing my heels into the horse's flanks, I took the lead. As we charged inland patches of green vegetation began to appear and the going became easier.

Our pursuers made no attempt to open fire. They realized what we were about and were endeavouring to close the gap. Even as I urged my mount on I could feel that the beast was beginning to flag. Its breathing was laboured. Spittle flew back at me.

Then, at last, we arrived at the base of the small hill. Bellowing out encouragement, I almost willed the poor beast up the slope. On reaching the summit I dragged a Colt Walker from its holster.

Christ, but it's heavy! I thought to myself.

I dismounted and rapidly made my dispositions. I sprinted over to Santa Anna and his delectable companion; I told them plainly what I expected.

'You will take no part in this. Hold the horses, and stay well behind us.'

The general had the good sense to acquiesce without comment. Together with two rangers he and Ana led the mounts down the gentle slope. Dismissing them from my mind, I turned my full attention on to the imminent encounter.

The proven rule was that untested and ill-trained infantry would always break before a determined cavalry charge. Unfortunately for the Mexicans we were neither untested nor untrained, and what followed was nothing short of slaughter.

With our horses out of harm's way fourteen of us dropped down on the crest. If we were to negate their numerical advantage, we needed to hit them hard and often.

Lee anchored the left flank whilst Tylee and myself took the right. That gave Kirby the freedom to prowl the line. He would regulate the volley fire, as he alone knew the names and abilities of all his men. All, except the naval lieutenant and myself, possessed single-shot percussion rifles. As the enemy pounded towards us I expected some rapid firing from that officer, but he seemed strangely restrained.

As the distance dropped below one hundred yards, Kirby gave the order to fire and eleven rifles, including his own, crashed out in unison. Yet still Tylee held off. At that range man and beast provided an excellent target. The strong wind whipped the smoke away, allowing me to witness the carnage. Eight animals tumbled to the ground. Some lay still, whilst others kicked out helplessly. Their riders, either stunned or injured, were effectively out of the fight.

The rangers discarded the empty rifles and cocked their massive revolvers. The Mexican troopers were brave men. Despite their losses they did not waver and continued to close on our position.

'Steady boys,' called out Kirby, somewhat unnecessarily. Having faced hordes of screaming Comanches, his men were unlikely to be intimidated by relatively civilized cavalry, but the sergeant couldn't resist his next remark. 'I'm the hard-case round here, not those manure spreaders.'

By way of support I unleashed the first barrel of my shotgun. The stock jarred my shoulder as its deadly load ripped forth. Peppered by shot, a heavily lathered horse stumbled, pitching its rider over its head. I cocked the second hammer and awaited the rangers' next volley. Again Kirby bellowed out the order and this time Samuel Colt's new weapons spat their defiance.

Exhilaration surged through me as I discharged the remaining barrel. There really was no finer experience than a one-sided battle. Before us, the effect of another well-aimed volley was visible for all to see. Four troopers had been smashed out of their saddles and there were more horses down, proving that the large-calibre handgun could indeed bring down both man and beast.

Looking to my right, I snapped at the naval officer in irritation.

'Are you in this fight, Mr Tylee?'

As though coming out of a trance he nodded curtly, then aimed at the still-advancing enemy. With a bang his repeating rifle discharged and a trooper was flung backwards off his mount. As though demonstrating his marksmanship, the lieutenant had deliberately chosen the smaller man over the larger horse.

I glanced down the line of rangers and noticed that some men were pushing the ramming arm back into place under the barrel of the Colt Walker before retracting the hammer. At Kirby's order, a third volley spewed lead and that proved to be enough. By some miracle the Mexican officer had survived and he possessed enough sense to know when he was beaten. Screaming out orders at his battered troop, he wheeled away from our position. I fully expected them to head back for the city walls at full pelt.

What actually happened took me by surprise and changed everything. As the rangers prepared to send another hail of .44-calibre balls after them the surviving troopers suddenly veered off to their left and swept round behind us. Their commander was out to salvage something from the debacle: our horses. The shock of recognition hit me like a hammer blow. If the Mexicans succeeded in running them off my mission was over and my humiliation would know no bounds. There was also the disquieting fact that one of the horse-holders counted for more than any number of army mounts.

I discarded the empty shotgun, grabbed the Colt Walker and scrambled to my feet. Such was the revolver's size and weight that it felt more like a diminutive carbine. Tylee was already careering down the reverse slope, bellowing at the startled horse-holders. If they stuck to their allotted task, which I prayed they would, then they would be completely defenceless. Desperately I bounded after the naval officer, at the same time cocking my unfamiliar weapon.

As the Mexican cavalry rounded the base of the rise they came into full view of Santa Anna's little band. With a collective roar of triumph the troopers charged towards them. Since they were armed with short-barrelled carbines called *escopetas* another one-sided contest was in prospect. I just prayed that their weapons weren't loaded with 'buck and ball', otherwise there would be indiscriminate slaughter of man and beast. Behind me, Kirby was exhorting his men to follow him down the slope, but I greatly feared that we were too late.

Yet, when it came, the gunfire was from a completely unexpected quarter. The heavy reports of two Colt Walkers resounded *behind* the troopers.

'By all the saints!' I mouthed joyfully. The firing had come from Travis and Davey – both of them fresh from a tooth-filling.

I came to a jarring halt, aimed my own revolver and fired it for the first time. With a reverberating crash it discharged. The recoil took me by surprise. The heavy ball caught a Mexican in his right shoulder and blasted him out of the saddle. Remembering Kirby's words of warning, I checked the ramming arm. Sure enough, it had dropped down from its seating.

The two latecomers fired again and two more of our

enemies' horses slewed sideways, throwing their riders. The remainder of their cavalry were now in amongst our horses. The situation was still truly desperate.

Then, as though suddenly seized by a manic fervour, Tylee began firing his eight-chambered rifle to deadly effect. Belatedly I realized that in the resultant mêlée our people were as much at risk as theirs. Which was possibly exactly what he wanted.

Under more sustained fire than they had expected, the Mexicans had faltered somewhat. So far we still held on to all of our mounts. Adopting a true parade ground tone, I bellowed:

'Lieutenant Tylee, you will stand down, *now.*'

Either the bugger did not hear me or he chose to ignore me. With great deliberation he aimed directly at Santa Anna. Then, almost unbelievably, he actually squeezed the trigger. Horror-stricken, I could only observe as two things happened next. His Excellency jerked like a marionette and released his hold on the reins. Then, directly behind him, a Mexican trooper vomited blood and slipped from his saddle.

Pure incandescent rage swept over me. I cocked my revolver and lunged towards Tylee. On reaching him I slammed the heavy barrel into the side of his head. With an anguished cry he slumped to the ground. Shaking with anger, I levelled my weapon at him. I truly believe that I would have shot him had not Captain Lee brusquely knocked it aside.

'We do not kill our own, Major Collins,' he stated in a calm but penetrating voice.

Our eyes locked and he stared long and hard at me. Gradually the fury inside me began to dissipate, to the point where I could actually regain logical thought.

'Very well,' I replied. 'But you will disarm this man and see that he does not leave this place. He is in your custody, Captain.'

Without waiting for any acknowledgement I returned to the fray, which, to my surprise, had actually ended. The Mexican troopers, or at least those who were able, had galloped off in disarray. Travis and Davey, being the only men mounted, had gone off in pursuit of Santa Anna's mounts. The rest of our horse herd was now safely in the hands of their individual riders. To my immense relief the general, although quite clearly distressed, was alive. His lover was bending over him, kissing his head and crying at the same time. As I approached, she suddenly turned on me and launched into a jumbled torrent of abuse, only some of which I understood.

First came rapid Spanish:

'*Qué pasa? Quita tu pinche cara de aqui*!' Then more lucidly, 'I saw it all. That *bastardo*, he try to kill *mi papa! Por qué?*'

My whole body seemed to go numb. 'Your father? But I, I thought he was your—'

'*Mi qué?* My husband? My lover? You men are all alike. You think everything is sex, sex, sex!'

Off to my left a ranger commented appreciatively: 'She's some *bronco*, that one.'

Her full-throated onslaught had left my mind befuddled. A nearby gunshot succeeded in partially clearing my head. Glancing around, I observed some of the rangers slaughtering the wounded Mexicans with either blade or ball, before gleefully relieving them of their possessions. Already brutalized by their relentless conflict with the godless heathens, such behaviour was quite normal for them.

At any other time I would have reprimanded them, but now I had just too many problems to confront. I turned back to Ana, struggling to think of something meaningful to say in her language.

'*Lo siento, señora,*' was what I finally managed to come up with.

As that was the limit of my rather pathetic linguistic capabilities I kneeled down next to her father. Tylee's rifle ball had struck the general's heavy bullion epaulette before ricocheting up into the Mexican trooper. Santa Anna had crumpled to the ground under the impact, whilst the trooper had died in considerable discomfort.

Santa Anna regarded me with an almost preternatural calmness. He tugged at the shattered epaulette.

'I am waiting for you to tell me that the *cochino* who did this is dead,' he remarked.

'No, he is not. But the man that he aimed at is.' Before he could protest I rounded on the two nearest rangers. 'Get this man on his feet, and on to his horse. Kirby, we need to get out of here.'

That individual was not in the least bit intimidated by my peremptory demand.

'Just as soon as Travis and Davey get back with the horses,' he replied calmly, I turned away and stalked back up the slope to where a now conscious Tylee waited with Captain Lee. Blood was seeping from the fresh cut on his face.

'You had no call to do that, English,' he barked, glowering up at me. Anger flared up within me again.

'You will address me by my rank, or as sir.'

'The hell I will! I could have you up before a drumhead court martial and shot for what you just did.'

Then it dawned on me what he was about. Clever. Very clever.

'I watched you attempt to kill General Santa Anna,' I told him. 'He is under the direct protection of General Winfield Scott. So it is you who will be court-martialled, Lieutenant.'

Tylee got shakily to his feet. Despite his obvious discomfort, the ghost of a smile appeared on his face.

'Show me the victim. Show me the witnesses.'

I shook my head in disbelief. This was ludicrous. I glanced

over at Lee.

'What did you see, Captain?' I demanded.

That individual had the good grace to appear embarrassed.

'With regret, Major, I cannot help you. I was looking to the horses. Without them our mission would be over.'

Gesturing over at Santa Anna I replied: 'Without him our mission would be over.'

The officer of engineers shrugged regretfully but remained silent. This was getting me nowhere. Time was passing. Turning momentarily to look back towards the city, I observed the survivors of the cavalry detachment streaming back to the city walls. A few stragglers limped back on foot, casting justifiably nervous glances in our direction.

Pounding hoofs signalled the return of our missing horses. Ranger Travis dismounted in front of me and spat out a stream of dark-brown tobacco. A lopsided smile played on his grizzled face.

'How do, Major? We leave you for five minutes and look at the trouble you get into, ha-ha-ha.'

Just what I needed, a humorous Texas Ranger.

'Very good Travis, very amusing. But you did well coming up behind them like that and recovering the horses.' As I looked at him I came to a decision. 'Kirby, give Lieutenant Tylee his horse. He is returning to Veracruz.'

An incredulous look spread over the naval officer's features.

'You can't do that. I've been assigned to you by the commanding general himself.'

'Tylee? What kind of name's that?' queried Travis. Now it was his turn to look puzzled.

Tylee took umbrage at such a question from a mere enlisted man.

'Hold your tongue,' he snapped. 'It's not for you to comment.'

He might as well not have spoken for all the notice that Travis took.

'Only I recall there was a fella of that name at the Alamo. And none of those men walked away.'

Thunderstruck, I stared at him. 'What are you saying?'

Travis's unkempt features contorted into a look of pity.

'I'm saying: there ain't many Tylees about. That one's dead. This one ain't.'

My wits had returned and with them a question.

'Where did that man hail from?' I asked.

'James Tylee came from New York, just like me.' Everybody's attention was now on the naval lieutenant as he continued: 'He was only thirty-six when that butcher killed him – and he didn't even get a Christian burial. There's not a day goes by without me thinking on that.'

I turned to face Lee. 'Surely you must agree that this changes everything?' I suggested.

The captain regarded me keenly.

'I agree that by rights General Santa Anna should be brought to account for his bad deeds,' he replied, 'but there is still no proof that this officer tried to kill him.'

Aware that time was passing I struggled to contain my anger. I felt as though there was a conspiracy building against me. Less than a day into the mission and I was beset by problems. Although still within sight of the coast, we were already surrounded by blood-soaked corpses. Violent death seemed to be a part of everything that I did. Yet such thoughts served no purpose. We needed to be gone. Tylee was right about one thing. He was with us at Scott's direct request and it would do little to aid my cause if I sent him back so soon.

'Very well. Lieutenant Tylee, you will remain with us under open arrest. Captain Lee will retain all your weapons and you will remain with him at all times.'

Anger suffused Tylee's features, but he managed to hold

his tongue. Ignoring him I continued: 'Sergeant Kirby, I want every man to reload his weapons and then mount up. We've been here long enough.'

'Damn right, Major!' he replied irreverently. 'Those greasers are starting to turn.'

CHAPTER FOUR

The afternoon sun burned down, with the wind off the Gulf doing little to deflect its power. As the column enjoyed a brief pause to rest the horses I took my last look at Veracruz. From high up in the hills that overlooked the city the view was breathtaking. Under normal circumstances the metropolis, with its walls and spires, would have been remarkable enough. But these were not normal times. The huge naval presence, although admittedly ominous, appeared to add to the city's grandeur. It seemed a genuine shame that so much destruction had to be wrought to obtain its surrender. The fact that the United States had only a dubious claim to be there at all did not make that any more palatable.

My thoughts switched to more pressing matters. What was so chilling about my current situation was that nobody, with the exception of Ana, had any interest in keeping her father alive. Even Robert Lee, a professional through and through, seemed to regard Santa Anna as fair game. The idea of an escort composed almost entirely of Texas Rangers seemed to border on lunacy.

Shuddering slightly, I took a furtive look around to see if I was being observed. Everyone appeared to be occupied, conveniently leaving the commanding officer to ponder his troubles.

I glanced over at Santa Anna's imposing though somewhat dishevelled figure. I couldn't imagine him benefiting his country or its people in any way, but then that wasn't the reason for our facilitating his return. And what of Ana de Luna? Since the apparent attempt on her father's life she had studiously avoided me, as though somehow blaming me. True, I was the officer in charge. Yet every ranger in my detail would probably have welcomed the chance to place a ball in Santa Anna's skull. Such animosity was natural under the circumstances, but did not help my peace of mind in the slightest. I spun round with the intention of addressing the column and found my way barred by the brooding figure of Sergeant Kirby. He was eyeing me speculatively, as though trying to make up his mind about something.

'There's one thing I just don't understand about this crackpot scheme. If that cockchafer needs to get back to his people, why don't we just turn him loose? He's already home.'

If nothing else his question showed that he had progressed beyond blind anger and had been giving some serious thought to His Excellency's presence amongst us. It illustrated why he had been chosen for promotion over his comrades. Therefore I favoured him with a considered response, rather than merely a glib answer to placate a subordinate.

'There are many people in this country – besides most of those in this detail – who would like to see him dead. He will only be truly safe with his own army at his back. To achieve that, he needs to reach Mexico City. Only then does President Polk's plan stand a chance. That is why I cannot risk taking another chance on Tylee. If he is out to avenge his brother, then it is my duty – and yours – to stop him, however much any of us may sympathize with him.'

The ranger took in a deep breath and then let it out in a rush.

48

'You really are between a rock and a hard place, ain't you?'

'As I said before, I really can't do this without you.'

A genuine smile lit up his weathered face.

'That's what I like about you, you're just so needy,' he replied.

Without affording me any chance to respond he swung round, clapped his hands together and called out:

'Travis, get the column saddled up. We got ground to cover.'

So we turned our backs on the coast and headed inland.

The rest of the day passed without incident. The rangers, used to the uncertainties of hostile territory, moved swiftly but with practised caution. Two riders were assigned point and rearguard duty. In addition, a third man was given a roving commission to ensure that we were not shadowed on our flanks.

I had quickly realized that the benefits of travelling through high ground outweighed the disadvantages. Although it made for harder going, there was little cultivation and therefore less chance of our meeting farmers and the like.

Determined to cover as much distance as possible, I kept our party on the move until the light began to drain out of the sky. Only then did I order a halt and with it the specific command that it should be a cold camp. The surrounding land might not be infested with Comanche warriors, but I had no intention of advertising our presence. Beef jerky and a single blanket would suffice.

Unfortunately such spartan accommodation proved to be unsatisfactory to His Excellency, as I soon found out. Still clad in his garish uniform, he limped over and favoured me with his most imperious expression. 'I have tolerated many indignities since commencing my journey with the *yanquís*, but this is beyond all reason.'

I gazed at him in genuine and total incomprehension. Frustrated, he tried again.

'When I lead a campaign I take with me only the finest delicacies. I eat off the finest plate, and sleep in a bed with only the—'

'Don't tell me,' I interrupted. 'With only the finest whores!'

Colour flowed into his face at an alarming rate as he struggled to find the words to express his outrage. Impatient to be done with such trivia I cast about me for a saviour. By great good fortune Ranger Travis had overheard our exchange. Unkempt and dishevelled as ever, he shambled over and placed himself squarely before the general. Gazing upon that self-obsessed personage, he gave vent to his feelings.

'I ain't got the learning that Colonel Jack or the major here got, but I know this. The only reason you're alive is because those two want it. And if you don't stop whining and bellyaching we're all going to forget that. Instead of thinking on which Dutch gal you could be poking, think on how much we want to make you bleed.'

With that Travis turned away, leaving Mexico's former ruler red-faced and speechless. To him, the common soldier ranked lower than a chicken, so to be so roundly abused in that way must have been mortifying. But Travis's forthright reproof had served its purpose. I had no further contact with the general that night.

The next morning found us on the move at first light. I intended to close on Xalapa that day and so would brook no delay. As we travelled ever higher through the hills, the coast seemed like just a distant memory. The increase in height would at least provide cooler air. So wrapped up in my own thoughts was I that I never actually heard the rider approach.

The sudden pressure of a hand on my left shoulder jerked me out of my reverie.

I turned to find, to my surprise, that Ana was next to me, so close that our knees were almost touching. From the expression on her face her arrival beside me boded ill. Her eyes held mine with a feverish intensity. I knew what was coming. Her father's remonstrations had failed, so she intended to try her hand.

'That *bastardo* Tylee. You saw what he did; yet still he lives. *Por que?*'

'What he did,' I replied patiently, 'was kill an enemy of his country. It was an act of war, nothing else.'

'You know what he tried to do and so do I,' she spat back at me. 'In my country that would be enough to have him executed.'

'He is a United States naval officer. He cannot just be shot out of hand. I cannot even prove beyond doubt that he tried to kill your father. Besides, if his brother was killed at the Alamo he has some justification.'

Painfully aware of her withering gaze, I took a stab in the dark. 'With a name like Tylee he could well be Irish – and those buggers live by the feud.'

'Buggers? Feud? I understand none of it.'

'Which is why you should keep out of the business of men.'

The anger on her face turned rapidly to a look of disgust.

'I had hoped for more from you, Major Collins,' she commented icily. Then she pulled her horse away.

Despite our acrimonious exchange I couldn't help but smile as I watched her retreat down the column. She was without doubt the most beautiful woman that I had ever encountered. From the expressions on the rangers' faces as she went past them I was not alone in my opinion.

The argument with Ana had actually served a purpose. It had

provided my mind with a diversion. Morning became afternoon and all remained peaceful. News of the invasion and the *yanquís*' impending advance inland must have spread, because our outriders did not encounter anyone. So engrossed in my thoughts was I that I failed to notice that we were approaching our destination until alerted to it by Robert Lee.

There, above and before us, lay the city of Xalapa, Santa Anna's birthplace. Known as the 'City of Flowers', because of the many wild varieties growing in the region, it also had the honour of being capital of the state of Veracruz. At over four thousand five hundred feet above sea level, Xalapa had grown up on a series of hills. Fortunately it had not been fortified. City walls do not just serve to keep people out; they can also act as barriers to keep other people in. From where I sat the most prominent building appeared to be the massive cathedral with its high bell tower. From there a keen-eyed sentry could spot anyone approaching the city. The question was: did the city have a garrison?

Lee had assured me that it did not, but it was some days since he had reconnoitred the district. I called over to that officer.

'Captain Lee,' I said, 'I would be very much obliged if you would take a closer look at the city. We don't want to stumble into anything. Your prisoner can stay with me.'

'Your servant, sir,' he replied. He pulled away from the column.

'You ain't fixing on taking us in there, are you?'

'I have little choice,' I replied, regarding Sergeant Kirby calmly. 'His Excellency desires a meeting with the *alcalde*. He needs to gauge the level of support that he may expect.'

'That son of a bitch is just using us to further his own ends. It ain't gonna set well with the men.'

I happened to agree with him, but I had little choice in the matter so my answer was deliberately awkward.

'Since when does an officer have to take into account the likes and dislikes of his subordinates?'

The furrows on the ranger sergeant's brow seemed to deepen into trenches as his eyes widened in astonishment. He edged closer, until I could almost taste his rancid breath. His voice was so soft that I had to strain to hear it.

'We got a saying back home that you might do well to get a handle on. "Don't piss down my back and tell me it's raining." '

Despite his parlous diction I took his meaning.

'Very well. The *alcalde* is the first Mexican of importance whom we have encountered since making landfall. From him Santa Anna could find out the whereabouts of the nearest troops loyal to him. Once he locates them we are free to go, so we must take a chance and accompany him into Xalapa. I don't like it any more than you do, but that's how it has to be.'

With that I held my peace to await Kirby's response. Before he had time to supply it Captain Lee presented himself before us. Looking every inch the professional soldier he calmly gave his report:

'Not wishing to create alarm, I did not penetrate the city streets. However, from what I could see there only appeared to be a few watchmen or constables present. No regulars or militia. I have to say that the layout of the city is not encouraging.'

That final sentence filled me with dread.

'Please elaborate, Captain.'

In a measured tone he continued: 'The city has expanded over a number of hillsides. Apart from the main plaza and certain other areas the streets are steep, narrow and winding. As you will have noticed there are no city walls, but the buildings have stout doors and much iron grillework. If we once got absorbed into that rabbit warren, I could not answer for the consequences.'

Instead of commenting I looked directly at Sergeant Kirby and gave an elaborate shrug. The experienced frontiersman knew exactly what I was thinking. Prudence dictated that we should avoid the city like the plague, yet I was duty bound to escort His Excellency wherever he chose to venture. With perfect timing that man now appeared before me.

'Major Collins, such delay. *No entiendo por qué.* I must talk with the *alcalde*, urgently. If I am to depose President Farias, I must know where his troops are and who commands them.'

Everything about the man revolted me and yet there was no avoiding the situation. In a voice loud enough for all to hear I said:

'Then my obligation is clear. We will escort you and your daughter into the main plaza.' Then, in a lower voice, I gave Kirby his instructions. 'We will enter the city in column of twos, flanking the general. Revolvers at the ready, but not cocked. I do not want to cause any unnecessary provocation.'

As he motioned his horse away to do my bidding I turned to Robert Lee.

'We, along with your prisoner, will take up the rear. I think it best that the good citizens see the general in all his glory first, rather than a United States Officer of Engineers.'

'As you will, sir,' he replied non-committally. He too doubted the wisdom of our advance, but as a career officer he knew better than to dispute it.

As my small force moved up the trail towards the outlying buildings there was a flurry of activity in the cathedral's bell tower. A sentry came into view as he bellowed out a warning in rapid Spanish. At the front of the column General Santa Anna waved graciously, for all the world like a victorious emperor returning to his subjects.

As we slowly threaded our way into the city proper people stopped to stare in amazement. There was no sign of any hostility, yet I could almost feel the tension in my men. It brought to mind an unwritten rule of the Comanche tribesmen far to our north. Retain mobility at all costs and never embark on urban warfare. That held true for the Texas Ranger force as well, which was at its best on horseback, getting in close to unleash hell with the aid of Samuel Colt's revolver. Yet here we were, voluntarily insinuating ourselves deep into a possible enemy stronghold, with neither a fallback position nor any reserves.

From all around us the citizenry came out of their adobe houses just to stand and gawp. It occurred to me that they had probably never seen *yanquis* before. The heat, which had eased off as we had climbed higher, came back to torment us now that we were surrounded by buildings. The buckskin-clad rangers gripped their weapons with sweaty hands, but kept them low over their saddles.

Eventually, after weaving our way through the uneven streets for some minutes, we found ourselves in the spacious main plaza. All Mexican towns were built around just such a large open area, which could be used for parades or ceremonies or simply for passing the time of day. This one contained the huge stone-built cathedral.

Directly facing us was what I took to be the main entrance, with the tower immediately to its right. Because of the way in which the ground fell away there were some two dozen steps leading up to its right-hand wall, with far fewer on the left. Strangely, as we progressed I noticed there was another, even more imposing and ornate entrance just behind the tower. This faced on to the plaza at an angle of roughly forty-five degrees. It was as though the Spanish, when constructing the edifice, had decided to provide their citizens with a choice of access points. Or possibly, in a country possessing a rigid caste system, it allowed for segregation.

A magnificent pediment had been built over each portico; one triangular, the other curved. As if all this grandeur wasn't enough, in the background, standing like a peaceful giant, was Mexico's highest peak: the snowcapped Pico de Orizaba.

The setting was quite splendid and for a moment it took my mind away from our truly precarious situation. My brief reverie was abruptly interrupted by a commotion at the far side of the plaza. Here, from an ornate residence of considerable substance, issued a number of gentlemen hastily arranging their clothing. Their style of dress was of the gaudy variety, much favoured by our temporary leader. With a great deal of fuss they advanced on His Excellency General Lopez de Santa Anna, with the apparent intention of paying him all due homage.

The spectacle was obviously too much for Ranger Travis. In a stage whisper, which travelled the length of the column, he made his feelings known to all.

'Look at them peacocks strut. What say we take a few of 'em down, boys?'

'Anyone cocks his piece, I'll take his trigger finger off with this here skinning tool.' Kirby's words had their intended effect. His ability with a knife was known only too well.

None of this banal exchange diverted Santa Anna one bit. He had dismounted with a flourish and was conversing with the foremost dignitary in rapid and expressive Spanish. After some minutes he gestured for me to join him. With a crowd of curious onlookers growing around us I was reluctant to dismount, yet I could not spurn such a direct invitation.

On foot, I made my way down the centre of the column. I was conscious of many pairs of eyes on me as I came level with the general. Was I viewed as a predatory *yanqui* invader, or as a benevolent foreign liberator?

If I had expected my first meeting with the *alcade* of

Xalapa to provide an answer to that question, then I was sadly mistaken. The man before me was quite obviously an expert dissembler. Swarthy, heavyset and with a distinct air of menace about him, he offered the traditional Mexican greeting:

'*Mi casa es su casa.*'

He followed this up with four words in heavily accented English:

'*Americano*, eat, drink, rest.'

When I protested that some clarification of our position was necessary, the *alcalde* merely shrugged his shoulders with apparent incomprehension and repeated:

'Americano, eat, drink, rest.'

Seemingly that represented the sum total of his linguistic abilities. I glanced over at Santa Anna.

'This will not stand,' I hissed. 'We are too vulnerable here. Just what has he told you?'

The general's expression displayed an alarming degree of complacency as he replied:

'I was born here. There is much loyalty to me. The *alcalde*, he must talk of my arrival with his *compadres*. We must all remain here and accept their hospitality to show good. . . .'

His fluency deserted him and he struggled to think of the right word. Returning my gaze to the inscrutable *alcalde*, I finished the sentence myself.

'Faith.'

That man regarded me through expressionless eyes, as he offered his own contribution:

'*Americano*, eat, drink, rest.'

By all that was holy, I had heard enough. I gave a slight bowing, then turned abruptly and walked away. Santa Anna called out to me and for the first time I detected a hint of anxiety in his voice.

'Major Collins, where do you go?'

Without stopping I called back:

'While you eat, drink and rest, I will see to my men. Sergeant Kirby.'

'Yo?'

'To me, please.'

As he joined me I lowered my voice. 'A blind man on a galloping horse could see that this is not right.'

The grizzled ranger regarded me steadily but remained silent, so I continued:

'Bivouac the men at that side of the plaza. Tether the horses somewhere close. See if you can occupy any of the buildings to use as cover. Only on their terms, mind. No force. Offer the good citizens a few coins. And no drinking!'

Kirby absorbed my instructions before offering his own suggestion.

'Why not just pull out now? These sorry-looking sacks of shit ain't gonna stop us.'

'And leave Santa Anna here?' I replied caustically. 'We might just as well have stayed on the coast and let him travel alone. Only those weren't our orders, were they?'

He produced a large sigh for dramatic effect before favouring me with a lopsided grin.

'Yeah, and you "bloody backs" are all for obeying orders, ain't you?'

Before I could reply he swung away and began barking out commands. He really was the most annoying subordinate imaginable.

As the light began to drain out of the sky I scrutinized my surroundings carefully. The vast plaza had virtually emptied of people; this, I presumed was due in some measure to our presence. Copious quantities of food and wine had been delivered to our temporary encampment, but I had ensured that the latter was strictly rationed. As Santa Anna and his daughter were enjoying the *alcalde*'s hospitality we numbered

58

eighteen. With only a slight suggestion of force Travis had obtained entry to a small *mercerias*. Its owners, who sold threads and buttons, had been persuaded to take a temporary leave of absence. Although far from being a strongpoint, it at least provided some cover in the event of things turning ugly.

As gloom descended on the state capital a number of citizens busied themselves lighting oil lamps. As they appeared around our portion of the perimeter I smiled appreciatively at them for the sudden illumination of our position. My thoughts, however, mirrored Robert Lee's expression. As the lamplighters departed I commented:

'Perfect for any sharpshooters, don't you think?'

The engineer glanced keenly over at me.

'And if I happened to be one, I'd be up in that bell tower,' he replied.

I considered him carefully before shaping my reply.

'I hope this night turns out to be entirely peaceful. But if it doesn't we will not be caught unawares. I deem it time for a council of war.'

Shortly after this exchange, Lee, Kirby, Tylee and myself gathered together in our newly acquired premises, away from the rest of the men.

'Gentlemen, His Excellency appears to be remarkably sanguine over his prospects in this fair city. I feel, however, that we may have quite possibly ventured into a "murder hole—". So what I intend is this: I will take Ranger Travis up into yonder bell tower, along with Mr Tylee's newfangled repeating rifle. From there, even in the murk, we should be able to observe any hostile advance on this position. Captain Lee, you will command here with Sergeant Kirby as your second. Should anything develop, fire only on my command.'

Kirby accepted his posting without demur. Although the officer of engineers was not part of the ranger's close-knit group, there was an air of calm authority about him that demanded respect. Tylee, however, had had enough.

'You take my rifle as though by right, and then reduce me to the ranks. I'll not—'

Peremptorily I cut him short. 'You forget, Mr Tylee, that you are still under open arrest. You cannot be reduced much further than that. And since I command here, I claim the right to appropriate any weapon as I think fit.'

Thereafter ignoring the lieutenant I turned to Lee.

'I suggest that you spread your men out with your backs to this building and, if time permits, dig in. Any questions?'

'Yeah,' replied Kirby. 'What the hell's "sanguine" mean?'

Chuckling, I stood up and called out to Ranger Travis.

'You are with me. Douse those lamps and collect as many as you can carry. Oh, and bring some lucifers.'

'Sounds like you're intending some mischief, Major,' Travis replied.

He couldn't have known just how prophetic that remark would turn out to be.

CHAPTER FIVE

As it turned out Travis was just able to carry six of the bulky oil lamps, whilst a single Colt Walker tested the limits of his belt. I, in contrast, was a walking arsenal. In addition to Tylee's rifle slung over my shoulder, I had a Holster Model Paterson Colt stuffed in my belt and a Colt Walker in each hand. Eager to try out the repeating rifle, I had elected to leave my shotgun with Kirby.

Ranger Travis, like his sergeant, was rather older than the average company recruit. Foul-smelling and uncouth, he was lacking in both intelligence and imagination, but in a fight he more than made up for those shortcomings.

In an attempt to distract the inevitable observers I had sent four supposedly very inebriated rangers off to the far side of the well-lit plaza, with instructions to start an exceptionally public brawl. That would also serve to confirm to whomever had issued the wine that their ploy had been successful. After all, everyone knew that *Americanos* were just drunken barbarians.

Leaving the others to dig in we cautiously moved towards Xalapa's cathedral. I intended to enter through the doors directly facing the rangers' position. Although darkness had fallen the sky was clear. An almost full moon bathed the city in its ghostly light, creating a perfect night for a Comanche 'murder raid', or an ambuscade by Mexican troops.

I stood under the portico of the immense building and waited for Travis to join me, silently praying that the noisy diversion had drawn off any sentries. So far no one had challenged us. My companion arrived, cursing under his breath at the sheer awkwardness of his load. Applying pressure to the handle, I eased open one of the heavy wooden doors. As the door fell back before us I was greeted by the strong smell of incense. To a – admittedly lapsed – Protestant, it was all the confirmation I needed that we were in a Catholic house of God.

Thankfully, the only illumination came from a few isolated candles. The enclosed steps up to the tower were on our right, through a small doorway. I gestured towards it and took the lead.

The scuffling noise that stopped us both in our tracks came not from above, but rather from somewhere behind us amongst the ornate icons. I spun round and cocked the vast revolver in my right hand. Travis, holding the cords to three lamps in each hand, was temporarily useless, so I moved past him. Desperately I scanned the vast interior for the source of the sound. If only it could turn out to be a rat.

Unfortunately, the loud click of my weapon's action had elicited a soft whimper. A small shrouded figure rose up near the altar. Beads of sweat suddenly coated my forehead as I struggled to identify any threat. Sounding far more confident than I felt, I called out: 'Show yourself!'

Hesitantly, the tiny shape inched towards me. The tension within me diminished slightly as I realized that it could only be a woman – or possibly a child. Yet the hood remained stubbornly in place.

'Show yourself,' I again demanded.

It shuffled to within a few paces of me before responding with one word, in what could only have been a feminine voice.

'*Quién?*'

What did she mean: 'who'? I could only be talking to her. Was the woman demented?

Conscious that Travis was now moving silently down my left flank, I suddenly surged forward and placed my gun muzzle under the edge of her hood, I swept the hood back over her head. Even by the meagre light of the candles, what I saw was enough to make me feel sick.

The face of the woman was covered in suppurating lesions and pustules. Such was the extent of the wreckage that it was impossible to guess at her age or even to discern whether she might once have been pretty. Involuntarily I took a step back. If she had wet leprosy I wanted no contact whatsoever.

Travis, observing closely from her right side, had little trouble in diagnosing her true condition.

'Them's syphilitic sores. This little lady likes the bucks. Ha! Bet she don't get many takers now, mind.'

Relief flowed through me, but it could not completely replace the revulsion that had taken hold. I had seen ill-used prostitutes before, but never one in such decay.

The problem now was what to do with her. Just to ignore her invited the possibility of her alerting the authorities in the hope of a reward. Remarkably, Travis's thought processes had kept pace with mine, yet his solution was one that I could not have even contemplated.

Having discarded the lamps he suddenly, without any warning, leapt behind the pathetic creature. Taking hold of her viciously by the hair, he yanked her head back. With practised speed a large knife appeared in his right hand. Such was the disparity of their strength that she could not even struggle. Before I could make any protest he cut deep into her exposed throat. Blood gushed over his blade as she simply died without a sound.

As though discarding a piece of refuse the ranger just

released her and stepped away. With her short life ended in an instant, the wretched individual collapsed on to the stone flags. From that point on she was no longer a person, but merely a carcass. So much for the sanctity of a church!

I was hardened to the face of warfare, but that brutal act against such a defenceless individual shook me to the core. My legs began to feel weak as reaction took hold of me. Travis, having wiped his blade clean on her clothing, regarded me curiously.

'You don't look so chipper, Major,' he remarked dispassionately.

'There was no need for that,' I managed to choke out. 'We could have tied her up, and left her 'til tomorrow.'

The ranger looked at me pityingly.

'She was dying anyhow,' he retorted. 'I just hastened it some.' As though to emphasize his point, he spewed out a stream of tobacco juice.

Faced with a *fait accompli* there was little that I could say or do. Time was passing and we needed to be up in the tower.

'Well at least drag her out of sight,' I told him, pulling myself together. 'If all this comes to nothing I don't want to be known as a common assassin.'

As he did my bidding I moved over to the bell tower and began a cautious ascent. If there were still anyone up there it would fall to me to deal with him. Travis had his hands full in more senses than one.

The steps were fashioned out of timber, slotted into the stonework and with a supporting frame. The width of the tower dictated that there should be a right-angled turn after every six steps, so that at one point I was directly above Travis as he huffed and puffed his way up with the heavy lamps. A thick rope dangled down from a circular hole in the tower's wooden floor. As I approached the open-sided bell chamber, I observed that the trapdoor was up, indicating the lack of a sentry.

So it proved. The only occupant of the tower was an ornate and highly polished bronze bell. As I waited for Travis to join me I peered cautiously over the edge of the low, outwardly curving wall. It was rather like being on a balcony, or in a box at the theatre. Even at night the vantage point afforded me a bird's-eye view. Directly in front of me I could make out the dark shapes of my men as they lay in their hastily dug trenches. The rest of the plaza's perimeter was well lit, so backlighting any targets that the rangers might be presented with. To my left was the *alcalde*'s residence. From there came muted sounds of revelry. Under different circumstances I would most happily have attended such a function, if only as an escort to the delectable Ana Leticia Arellano de Luna.

Such impractical thoughts were abruptly banished by the arrival of my sweating, cursing subordinate.

'That afflicted bitch'll start to turn come morning. It'll be hell up here if we ain't gone by then.'

I gazed at him balefully.

'And what if the priest finds her before then?' I asked. He returned my stare.

'Ain't likely. I kilt him too!' he snapped back.

My eyes widened in shock, but before I could remonstrate he began to chuckle.

'Don't get into a conniption fit. I was just joshing with you. I weren't raised to lie. Besides,' he drawled, glancing casually over the rear wall, 'If those fellas mean business, it won't matter what he finds.'

With the vast bulk of the cathedral behind us, the approaching force would not be in view for long. There was time enough though to confirm my worst fears. The dark hue of the uniform coats was insufficient to conceal so large a detachment. As the men flowed slowly through the winding streets the silvery moonlight glistened on their weapons.

Obviously not expecting to be viewed from above, they had not taken the trouble to blacken them.

It was difficult to assess their exact number, but there were certainly in excess of fifty and possibly as many as one hundred. They obviously knew exactly where to find their prey. Their current course would bring them out on the far side of the plaza, directly opposite my men. With our religious citadel interposing, the intruders would be able to get in close before making their move.

Even under the stress of the moment it occurred to me that in truth *we* were actually the intruders and that they were most likely the legitimate federal authority. Then again, the benefit of having Santa Anna present was that I could leave the politics to him – if he survived the night. Because those *soldados* could well have been coming for him, just as much as for us. We didn't have much time.

'Ranger Travis, if you value the lives of your friends down there, get all those lamps burning.'

The man glanced at me sharply before attending to the task.

'Thank Christ for lucifers!' he muttered.

I placed my two large-calibre revolvers on the floor and recovered Tylee's rifle from behind my back. As a body of men began to accumulate below I became aware of a warm glow in the tower and prayed that it did not alert the enemy. If they acted as I had expected and remained in the shadows on either side of the cathedral, then we would avoid discovery.

Cautiously, I stole a glance over the left-hand wall. Its curvature afforded me a bird's-eye view of the soldiers clustered directly below me. They had got into position directly opposite the rangers and were now presumably awaiting the command to attack. I had to assume that the same was happening on the other side of the building. Lee's men were dug in and must by now be aware of the approaching force. I felt certain that, as a consummate professional, he would await my orders, regardless of any developments. So, it was now or never!

I turned back to Travis. 'You're promoted to grenadier,' I hissed at him. 'Heave three of those lamps over this wall. Sharply now.'

Grinning with pleasure at my lethal scheme, he carried the lamps to my side, extended his arms and simply let go. I was already leaning over the edge, clutching Tylee's rifle. As the oil-filled lamps dropped I cocked it, aware that what I had just instigated was the nearest thing to an act of God that I was likely to unleash that night. I had no reason to suspect that it was only the start of it.

The three bombs landed, causing total surprise, on a tightly knit mass of men. Two of them struck the tall cylindrical military caps known as shakos, whilst the third smashed into the hard-packed earth. As the oil ignited two men simultaneously found themselves on fire and in unimaginable agony. As their screams echoed throughout the plaza their comrades milled around in shock. I took swift aim with Tylee's rifle and squeezed the trigger.

The first chamber detonated with a roar and down below a soldier crashed to the ground. At that range and with so many illuminated targets I just could not miss. I cocked my piece and fired again – and again and again. Wreathed in powder smoke, with my ears ringing both from the discharges of my weapon and the screams of my victims, I felt a familiar surge of exhilaration flow through me.

My next shot caught a soldier in the top of the head. The lead ball exited through his jaw, blood and bone fragments flying everywhere. With five chambers discharged I was on the point of firing again when, from near the cathedral's entrance, there came a thunderous bellow of command.

'Get your feckin' arses to me, *now!*'

It wasn't the words but rather the accent that seized my attention. My earlier remark to Ana about the Irish had just returned to haunt me.

Alarmed, I pulled back from the edge and turned to Travis.

'How can this be? Are they our allies?'

He made short shrift of my concerns.

'The hell they are! Them cockchafers are San Patricio's.'

His brief but direct description explained everything. The Batalion de San Patricio was the Mexican name for the Saint Patrick's Battalion. Hundreds of Irish-born immigrants, disenchanted with their treatment by Anglo Protestant officers in Zachary Taylor's army of the north, had deserted to join the Mexican cause. They considered their motive to be just, but to the American forces they were nothing but despicable traitors, loathed and feared and fit only for the hangman's noose.

If left to his own devices their leader would soon rally his flank. After commanding Travis to heave his remaining oil lamps over the front wall, I yelled over to the ranger detachment:

'San Patricios, Lee. Do your worst!'

Almost instantaneously a fusillade of shots sounded below. A blizzard of masonry chips flew into the air and I dropped to the floor to protect my face. Then, with marvellous timing, a seamless volley crashed out at the edge of the plaza. I had no doubt that the rifle fire, aided by the temporary lamplight, would be accurate. More screams resounded in the night and I took my chance. Leaning over the front wall this time, I discharged two more chambers to good effect. There could be no question that an element of the San Patricios was reeling under our combined assault, but we were still heavily outnumbered and there were signs that their own discipline was taking effect. Nearly all the soldiers on their right flank had dropped flat, and were beginning to return fire. Moreover their officer, whose voice had enabled us to identify them, was turning his attention on to our high redoubt.

'Sergeant Devlin. Get some of your boyos into dat church. No damage, mind! Remember what it is.'

Chancing my luck one more time, I sighted down the barrel on to the torso of that voluble individual and squeezed the trigger. He was obviously under the protection of his god that night, because there came a loud pop as the percussion cap detonated, then . . . nothing. *Hangfire!*

In that state the rifle was of more danger to me than the enemy and I didn't have the time to set about removing the nipple to gain access the chamber. Cursing my luck, I tossed the heavy weapon over the wall like so much rubbish.

Unburdened of his flammable liquids, Travis had drawn his Colt Walker and was poised above the trapdoor. His expression was grim.

'I reckon them stairs'll be swarming with bogtrotters before long. If they fire the place, you and me is paroled to Jesus.'

'Not very likely. Remember, this is a Catholic church. If they do, well, we're already halfway there.' Without giving him the chance to reply to my witticism, I continued: 'Besides, we're going to do the last thing they would expect. We're going to attack.'

'The hell you say!'

Yet my reasoning was unassailable.

'If we stay here we will surely die. Out in the open we stand a chance and anything we do helps Lee and the others. Now, stand aside. I'll take us down.'

Travis shrugged and then did as he was told. Having cocked both weapons, I lowered myself through the trapdoor. If the Almighty preserved me from any more misfires I had seventeen chambers available, which was an enviable amount of firepower for one man.

Carefully I made my way back down the tower. Even with all the gunfire going on in the plaza, I was still able to over-hear snatches of a heated dispute in the cathedral.

'Sure an' you're a fine man, Sergeant, sending us up dere. Wit dem after waiting to gun us down like dogs!'

'Eejit, dere's only feckin' two o' dem!'

'*Pog mo thoin!*'

After that unfathomable comment I lost interest. I leapt down the stairs two and three at a time, desperately hoping to close with them before they got organized. Even in the fear and exhilaration of the moment I was aware that Travis was following closely behind. Praying that I didn't lose my balance, I endeavoured to keep both gun muzzles pointing roughly towards the tower entrance. As I reached the final right-angled turn a dark figure appeared in the doorway. With his eyes wide as saucers he cried out:

'Bleeding hell, it's dem!'

They were the last words that he uttered in this world. Coming to a juddering halt, I pointed the long barrel of my right-hand Colt Walker down at his chest and squeezed the trigger. In such a confined space the detonation was tremen-dous. My ears rang and powder smoke blanketed the scene. The unfortunate soldier was gone.

I jumped straight over the remaining stairs down to ground level. Praying that the ramming arm had not dropped from its seat, I cocked the revolver. The large cylinder revolved smoothly on its cylinder pin, placing another lethal chamber in line with the gun barrel. There was a flurry of activity around the entrance and two shots rang out. They could only have been fired for effect, as neither of the balls came anywhere near me and the resulting smoke just added to the confusion.

Knowing just how precarious our situation was, I was deter-mined to keep the pressure up. Travis had arrived at my side, so I put out my arm to hold him in check. With my best parade ground voice I bellowed out:

'Come on, men. Let's finish the bastards!'

Then I let rip with both revolvers. Taking his lead from me, Travis also fired his revolver into the throng. The noise within the base of the tower was simply indescribable. The sheer density of the powder smoke had temporarily concealed us. I knew then that we had a brief moment of opportunity to follow the skirmishers' maxim of 'fire and move'. We were both temporarily deafened, so I nudged Travis and beckoned him on. I burst into the main body of the cathedral and sprinted away from both of the large doorways. Had we attempted to fight our way through either of them we would as likely have been shot by our own men as by the San Patricios.

I searched frantically for another exit, cursing the fact that I had not reconnoitred the building earlier. More shots rang out, but again they were wide of the mark. It was Travis who saved the day. While looking for somewhere to conceal the girl's body he had discovered a small rear door. He told me of this and took the lead. I pounded along the stone flags behind him, dreadfully aware of my vulnerability to musket fire. With any luck our way out would allow us to approach the *alcalde*'s residence, which had to be our next destination. I had no idea of Santa Anna's situation, but I was duty bound to find out what it was. If we left the building with our pursuers close behind we would be on open ground and in serious trouble.

'Travis,' I yelled, 'we need to hit them again before we go out there.'

'Dang right!' he snarled. The brutalized ranger was not always quick on the uptake, but in combat he knew exactly what was required. Near the door was a large solid table upon which were set various religious icons. Faced with harsh

71

necessity we heaved this over to serve as a barricade.

The debatably traitorous Irish contingent now numbered around a dozen and had regained some semblance of order. Utilizing whatever cover they could find, they began to loose off a disciplined musket fire in our direction. They could afford to bide their time, whilst we could not. As we crouched down behind the heavy screen large-calibre balls began to chip splinters out of it. I turned to Travis.

'We need a diversion,' I stated.

'So torch the place,' he replied nonchalantly. 'Cremate the whore and any other son of a bitch we can catch.'

The idea of desecrating a church horrified me at first, but then I began to appreciate its charms. It would smoke out our assailants and create havoc amongst their comrades. Caught between accurate rifle fire and a blazing cathedral, they would have little choice but to retire.

I squeezed off a shot.

'Right, let's do it,' I yelled back. 'Set that tapestry afire and throw it over the pews. I'll cover you.'

Whilst I maintained a steady fire Travis ripped the wall hanging down and held it over a candle. The material must have been bone dry because combustion was almost instantaneous. Darting out into the nave he hurled it on to the pews. The wood must also have been tinder dry, because tongues of flame were soon licking over the rows of seating. The fire spread with gratifying speed.

Mortified cries came from the Irish.

'Dem bastards are after burning us all.'

Travis laughed out loud as he surveyed the wanton destruction. His pitiless reaction prompted a cry of rage:

'May the devil choke you!'

This imprecation had no effect on my subordinate. Yet, as though by divine retribution, it was then that the ranger made a fatal error.

Instead of dropping down and using the available cover he whirled round and raced back towards me. Powered by a relatively low muzzle velocity, the one-ounce soft-lead ball caught him in the upper left arm, almost severing it from his body. With his features registering uncomprehending shock, he stumbled the final few paces, before collapsing next to me. Pain hadn't actually hit him yet, but blood was pumping from the ghastly wound. With the bone completely shattered, the limb was hanging by mere skin and muscle.

If he was to have any chance of survival a tourniquet was required instantly, but at that crucial moment the San Patricios within the church decided to launch a determined assault on our position. With flames now taking an unstoppable hold on the interior, it would be their one chance to finish us.

I bellowed at Travis to fire if he could, then I reluctantly turned away to face the onslaught. A red-haired moustachioed sergeant had bullied his men into abandoning their cover. Advancing at the run, in their blue tunics and less than white trousers they presented me with outstanding targets. If only I had not left the 'two-shoot' gun behind. Remaining crouched behind my barrier, I levelled both revolvers and fired. Slivers of copper sought out my eyes as I was enveloped in pungent smoke. High-pitched screams testified to my accuracy. I now had two chambers remaining in my left-hand Colt and one in the right-hand one. And, of course, Travis's revolver. There had to be at least four in that.

As the smoke thinned I again cocked my pieces. The San Patricios were brave men. Despite their losses they continued to close on me. There was only time for one more volley. My muzzles almost touched the nearest pair as I squeezed the triggers. With a crash the chambers discharged. Both of my victims were struck in the upper torso, their tunics set afire by the muzzle flashes. At such close range the balls hit with the

73

force of a sledge-hammer, smashing the men back into their comrades. Yet there were other men who managed to avoid the crush and my time appeared to be running out.

Volley fire would have finished me, yet not a man amongst them stopped to aim his musket. Their single-shot muzzle-loaders couldn't all have been empty. Flanking both sides of the table, they seemed intent on physically tearing me apart; such was their desire for revenge. Grimy brutalized faces loomed before me.

Then, from the floor to my right, came an unexpected crash as Travis fired his revolver. The ball took his victim in the throat, so that the man died choking on his own blood. A look of stunned surprise was etched on his features. I threw my empty right-hand revolver at another face, then whipped out my long-bladed knife.

Cold steel is the ultimate last-ditch defence, almost primeval in its ferocity. Slicing it before me in a horizontal arc, I carved across the bridge of my nearest assailant's nose. With a scream of pure agony he fell back, his shako tumbling to the ground. From beside me came another thunderous report as the ranger fired again. Bellowing out an obscene challenge, I wielded my knife back and forth like a berserker from the Dark Ages. As it struck again and again I could feel a warm sticky liquid splash on to my face. I screamed out my defiance and continued to brandish the blade in all directions. I cannot recall how long I maintained that level of aggression. Certainly, I was too far gone in my own bloodlust to notice that the cutting edge was no longer connecting.

Then, with a jolt, I suddenly realized that we were all alone. The few survivors of that frantic bloodletting had scurried back towards the main entrance. The San Patricios were used to dealing with hard men, but a madman was an altogether different proposition. In addition, the whole interior of the cathedral was now ablaze. The heat was intense. Anything that

74

could burn was burning. It would only be a matter of time before the flames reached the roof supports.

Now that the fighting over, at least temporarily, a desperate weariness came over me. I longed to just collapse on the ground. My mouth felt parched and not only from the heat. I sheathed my bloodied knife and twisted round to examine my companion. With a searing shock, I stared into his lifeless eyes. They regarded me unblinkingly and I had to make a conscious effort to tear my glance away. The whole of his left side was soaked with blood and more of the stuff, along with a seasoning of dark-brown juice, trickled out of his mouth and nostrils. Even with death claiming him he had managed to keep firing. That, as much as my wild posturing, had turned the tide for us.

The knowledge that I had to get out of there and in so doing leave him to the flames pained me more than I would have believed possible. I reached down and gently removed the heavy revolver from his grasp. Swiftly I examined the percussion caps and discovered that there were two chambers charged; where I was going I would probably need them. The Colt Walker that I had hurled from me in desperation could stay where it lay.

Backing watchfully away from the scene of carnage, I cocked both revolvers yet again. As usual I raised them vertically, so allowing any fragments of the spent percussion caps to fall out, away from the intricate mechanisms.

I opened the small arched door with care and escaped gratefully into the fresh night air. Although I had no religious leanings I fervently prayed for there not to be a rearguard. The lack of one proved that our foes were overly confident in their numbers. They had not expected to have to cover a retreat. There was no peace to be had however. From the front of the cathedral came the sound of heavy gunfire. The rangers were obviously using their Colts to stand off some increasingly desperate assaults. Then I heard a deeper explosion, instantly recognizable as the two barrels of my shotgun being detonated at once.

My natural inclination was to hit the San Patricios in the rear, but it could not be. I had to find Santa Anna and his daughter. The *alcalde*'s residence was just in view, off to my right. Not surprisingly, the lamps outside it had also been extinguished. Although no sentries were visible I decided against a direct approach. I turned roughly forty-five degrees to my right and trotted over to the edge of the plaza. Every building appeared to be securely locked and shuttered against the outside world. Not a flicker of light showed anywhere, yet as I crouched there in the darkness, I could almost feel the sticky unease of the residents closeted in their airless rooms.

Damn them all! I reflected irrationally. *We didn't ask to be set upon.* But then we hadn't been invited into their country either.

I placed my revolvers carefully on the ground and vigorously wiped a pair of sweaty palms on my trousers. Over at the cathedral the flames had taken the main doors and a fierce light now bathed the area in front of it. From the ranger's position came a high-spirited yell followed by:

'God damn! We're blowing this town all to hell.'

For the remaining San Patricios the situation must have seemed disastrous. Indeed, the musketry was now slackening off. Still, there was no escaping the fact that I would have to find His Excellency myself. Time was passing and my failure to do so would mean that all the bloodshed had been for nothing.

I collected up my weapons and stealthily moved towards the large building. As would be expected, there was a respectful distance between it and the nearest dwellings. From the nearest available cover I observed the substantial two-storey residence. I had a stark choice before me. I could either burst in through the front door and take my chances, or stumble off into the void around the rear, searching for another way in. Neither option was enticing.

Thoughts of the fearful struggle in the cathedral and of Travis's brutal demise crowded in on me. With them came anger. I wasn't going to skulk anywhere. I was going through the front door and God help anyone who tried to hinder me. With a disdain for danger that bordered on lunacy I rose up to my full height and stepped forward. Looking neither left nor right, I walked steadily over to the ornate double doors. The thought that they might be locked never occurred to me.

Which is, of course, exactly what they were.

'A pox on these people!' I fumed.

Refusing to countenance any obstruction, I eased the hammer on my left-hand Colt down to half cock. Then I reversed the weapon and hammered on the door with the butt.

No response.

Again I pounded the timber; this time there came a reaction of sorts.

'*Marcharse!*'

Whatever that meant, the doors remained closed to me. Simple anger became transformed by frustration into an incandescent rage, which threatened to overwhelm me. A red mist formed over my eyes. I had survived vicious hand-to-hand fighting in what was now a charnel house, only to be baulked by a mere popinjay. It would not stand!

I bellowed back:

'I am a British mercenary. Your cathedral is ablaze by my hand. If you do not surrender General Santa Anna immediately, this *mansion* will also burn. Everybody within will be put to the sword. Gold is all that I recognize. I care nothing for the lives of anyone in this miserable country.'

From within there came the sound of a heated argument. With relief, I recognized the sound of Santa Anna's voice. Behind me the firing was dying away, enabling me to hear the sound of footsteps as they approached the doors. Santa Anna's heavily accented tones reached me through the timber.

'They say that you are the very devil, Major Collins. No ordinary mortal would seek to destroy a house of God.'

Quick-witted as ever, he was obviously playing his part in my charade, so I replied swiftly.

'I recognize no God, only mammon.'

There was more jabbering in Spanish, before at last a door was unbolted. I stepped sharply back and levelled both revolvers. The door opened sufficiently to allow passage for the general. No sooner was he out than it slammed shut. The remaining occupants really didn't want anything to do with me. Whatever they had hoped to gain by their plot seemed suddenly unappealing to them.

His Excellency appeared totally unruffled by his temporary captivity. However, on looking at me directly he could not help flinching slightly. I realized that the streaks of blood across my face must have given me a somewhat hellish appearance. Yet his praise was generous.

'You are an officer without equal. To have—'

I demanded his silence. There were other matters to consider. Highlighted by the flames, we were awfully vulnerable to an assassin's ball. I took him him firmly by the arm and led him into the shadows at the edge of the plaza. Something else was bothering me.

'Where is your daughter?'

Anxiety clouded his features as he regarded me intently.

'She slipped away when the shooting began. Surely she is with your men?'

'I truly hope so,' I replied earnestly. 'I have been separated from them for some time.'

An eerie calm had settled over the plaza. True, there sounded the moaning of wounded men and the fierce crackling of burning wood, but the violent detonations had ceased entirely.

Not wishing to die by friendly fire, I called out:

'Kirby?'

'Hey.'

'I've got the general. We're coming in.'

The sight that met my eyes was truly horrendous. There had been a fearful amount of violence. In front of the blazing cathedral there lay possibly two score broken bodies. The large-calibre lead balls, fired at close range, had devastated flesh and bone. The wounded lay untended, crying out for water, for their mothers, or simply for the relief of death.

The Texas Rangers, lying in shallow trenches, had fared differently. Their casualties, though far fewer in number, had nearly all taken headshots, with fatal results. From what I could see at least half a dozen young rangers would not be returning north of the border.

Kirby, powder-stained and belligerent as ever, greeted our return with:

'What is it with you and fires?'

'It was . . . expedient.'

'Whatever it were, the greasers ain't gonna like it. They got religion down here.'

'Could you have stood the Irish off without us, Sergeant?'

His grimy face produced the makings of a smile, which just as quickly vanished as he looked past us.

'Where's Travis?'

Feeling almost physically sick, I pointed at the war-torn house of worship.

'He didn't survive that,' I replied.

A cocktail of rage and sorrow engulfed the ranger

sergeant's features. He had doubtless seen it all in his time, but such a development was altogether too much.

'Well, that just tears it! That man was a dumb, ornery son of a bitch, but he was my friend.'

He cast around for someone or something to take his anger out on and his eyes inevitably settled on Santa Anna. Knowing exactly what was about to happen, I stepped briskly between the two men. Sure enough, Kirby's knife had appeared in his hand.

'Step aside,' he snarled.

I stood my ground and attempted to deflect his anger by asking a question.

'Where is Ana?'

Before he had a chance to respond there was a muffled boom from somewhere beyond the city limits. Officer of Engineers Robert Lee knew exactly what that portended.

'Everybody down,' he yelled.

The urgency in his voice registered with us and we all dropped to the ground. From the midst of the dead and wounded San Patricios there came a loud thump, followed by a massive explosion. Sections of jagged metal from the exploded shell flew everywhere, slicing into the unfortunate soldiers. Such a weapon could not discriminate between friend and foe.

If the enemy were prepared to bombard their own city we stood no chance. We needed to get into open country, fast. I leapt up, hauled Santa Anna to his feet and bellowed out a command.

'Take everything and go!'

The horses had been tethered in an alley close to hand. In the mad scramble to reach them I endeavoured to keep myself between the general and Kirby, although the sergeant's anger appeared to have dissipated under the demands of self-preservation. Thinking ahead, I insisted that all the riderless animals be brought along as well. There was no foretelling what the future might hold for us.

As we mounted up Captain Lee demonstrated just how calm and collected he could be under pressure by taking the time to answer my earlier question.

'You should know, Major, that the *señora* disappeared some time ago . . . along with Lieutenant Tylee.'

Behind us, there came a tremendous crash as part of the cathedral's roof collapsed. It seemed a fitting backdrop to Lee's deeply unwelcome news.

All in all it had been one hell of a night!

CHAPTER SIX

The new dawn found us camped on the reverse slope of a ridge overlooking the city. Although the cathedral was out of sight, it was impossible to ignore the pall of smoke that hung over it in the morning sky. The consecrated building would surely be just an empty shell by the end of the day.

Our party was much reduced. Of the original fourteen rangers, seven were now dead, including the long-serving Travis. Following our rapid departure a few more shells had exploded in the plaza, but only the dead were abroad to witness them.

For the remainder of the night we had slept, with only one man at a time standing guard duty. After what had taken place in Xalapa immediate pursuit was unlikely. As Kirby had remarked: 'We dealt 'em a crippler, boys!'

With the coming of daylight I had many questions in need of answers and His Excellency was first in line. I was aware that, quite naturally, all he wanted to discuss was his daughter's whereabouts, but there was more at stake than just her survival.

'How could the San Patricios have arrived so swiftly?' I asked him.

'They were already here,' he replied, regarding me impatiently. '*Con artilleria también*. Waiting for your General Scott to advance from the coast.'

I persisted. 'And what did the *alcalde* seek to gain by taking you prisoner?'

Now I had his full attention.

'That *bastardo*, he think to present me in irons to the monarchists. Those fools wish to install a king, or even rejoin the Spanish Empire. That is all I fought against. They know they can never be secure whilst I take breath. Well, I will punish such disloyalty.'

That seemed a trifle rich considering that Farias and not he was the serving president, but I was given no time to mull it over.

'I was born here. Xalapa is my true *casa*. These are my people and they will suffer for this.'

Thinking about the charred cathedral and the plaza full of body parts, I decided that they probably already had. It also occurred to me that a country permanently riven by dissent could never repel a well-organized invasion force. Yet voicing my opinions would have changed nothing in that man's mind, so I excused myself and sought out Messrs Lee and Kirby.

'I believe we should break our fast and then move on from here,' I said, addressing them both. 'If those deserters were stationed near by, then there may be some mounted units as well.'

Before I could continue Robert Lee spoke out.

'Then, with regret, you will have to continue without me, Major Collins. My orders were to guide you as far as this city and then return to the coast.'

I stared at him in amazement. After all that had taken place the previous night, such an announcement was the last thing that I had expected. Yet, regarding him closely, I realized that he was only doing his duty as he saw it.

Curbing my annoyance, I responded with an earnest entreaty.

'Disaster has befallen us. You must see that. There were twenty of us when we left Veracruz and now we are eleven. I need every man who is able to hold a gun and this mission takes precedence over your staff duties. What I – we – are trying to achieve is at the express wish of the commander in chief.'

I paused to give him time to absorb my remarks. Then something else occurred to me. 'You must also now agree that Lieutenant Tylee has, by seizing the general's daughter, jeopardized everything that those seven Texas Rangers died for. The only thing that can await him on our return is a court martial. *If* we ever see him again.'

'Oh, he'll turn up again,' drawled Kirby. 'He's got something to bargain with now. Just depends on how high we rate his hand.'

Replying instinctively and without real consideration, I said, 'I'm sure her father would give his life to ensure her safe return.'

The sergeant favoured me with a cynical smile. 'Do tell. You got more faith in that son of a bitch than I have. Besides, her being back alive with him dead would kind of upset your plans. 'Fess up, Major!'

As usual there was a remorseless logic to his mangled patois. Throughout this exchange Lee had observed me closely. Then, having given my plea careful thought, he stated his position.

'I believe you have the right of it, sir. I will remain with you until General Santa Anna has been safely delivered to Mexico City, or until you release me.'

Relief swept through me. I was on the point of declaring my thanks when I was rudely interrupted. Santa Anna, noticeably sweating in his full-dress uniform, had been observing our discussion. His impatience had mounted until he could no longer contain himself.

'Enough of this! What about my *hija*, my Ana? We cannot just leave her out there, with that accursed *yanqui*. Someone must search for her.'

Kirby had heard enough. 'Do tell. And which Yankee's gonna do the looking? Then again, you was born here. Bain't you up to it?'

The aristocratic Mexican gazed stonily at his lowborn tormentor, yet remained silent, allowing the ranger to continue.

'Tylee's gonna be out there watching us right now, but it's you he wants, not her. Leastways I reckon it is. Not that it matters. He could rape her and still do a trade!'

Santa Anna always had to struggle with the ranger's English, yet he had caught enough of this. With a roar of anger he reached for his pepper-box pistol. Knowing that he could not possibly survive an encounter with Kirby, I again placed myself between the two men. The almost routine need to do so was getting tiresome.

If our situation had not been so precarious I might well have appreciated the truly outstanding scenery. We were making good time on our journey to Perote, the next settlement of any size on the way to the capital. High up in the hills, with the morning air comparatively fresh, a fine day beckoned, yet its magic was lost on us all. The previous night had taken too heavy a toll. Seven sons of Texas, strong and true, would not be returning home to the twenty-eighth state.

And how had they died? Defending their families from marauding Comanches? Apprehending dangerous *pistoleros*? No, their lives had been squandered protecting a corrupt and venal former dictator, solely bent on recovering his tainted throne.

My thoughts turned to more practical matters. What could Ana have been thinking, allowing herself to be carried off by Tylee? Quite possibly she had been given no choice. He was a powerful, well-made young man and the rangers had doubt-less been fighting for their lives.

From just behind me Kirby's voice cut in with an almost uncanny remark.

'He ain't gonna like it none, you losing his newfangled rifle and all!'

I took his meaning, but chose to be deliberately obtuse.

'All what?'

There were times when I just longed to hear the English language spoken correctly. The bastardized version favoured by those colonials was, at times, really just too awful to bear. This was one of those times.

Yet Kirby was having none of it.

'Don't get ornery with me, you black-hearted English cockchafer!'

His response took me completely by surprise, but then inevitably raw anger began to surge through me. Brutally reining in my horse, I twisted in the saddle to reprimand him.

'I could have your stripes for such blatant insubordination, *Sergeant*!'

Completely contrary to expectations, a wry smile appeared on his weathered face.

'Mighty handy I ain't wearing any then, *sir*!'

Before I had time to respond to that he continued: 'And don't it feel better to breathe some fire? A conniption fit kind of sets you up.'

I could feel my jaw drop. The man was incorrigible and yet I now perceived his real purpose.

'Very well, Kirby. You've made your point, but don't go making a habit of it.'

The man flipped his slouch hat by way of acknowledge-ment before moving off down our much-reduced line.

We had by now left Xalapa well behind and were again heading west towards the nation's capital city. Moving swiftly, we had managed to avoid any further contact with the Saint Patrick's Battalion, which entirely suited me. They had proved to be a determined and aggressive foe and we could not afford another such victory.

Although my black mood had lifted I was still no nearer to finding a solution as to how to prise Ana out of the naval officer's clutches.

As it turned out, I could have saved myself a lot of anxiety. Kirby had been quite correct. Lieutenant Tylee gained no benefit by remaining elusive. However, his method of confirming this both shocked and aroused me.

Evening was upon us. We had made good progress and my thoughts had turned to finding a sheltered and defensible campsite for the night. The ranger assigned to point duty trotted his horse into view and then held his position, awaiting our arrival. His rejoining the column indicated that he had something to report.

I knew nothing of the man other than his name, Rance Buckner. He was in his twenties and bearded, as so many of them were. As we got nearer I noticed the expression on his face as he gazed at his sergeant. There was excitement to be sure, but something else as well.

As I reined in next to Kirby, Buckner reluctantly turned to me.

'You'd better come see this, Major. It sure beats all.'

In spite of the tropical warmth a chill swept through me.

'Captain Lee, I would be obliged if you'd ensure that the general remains to the rear at all times.'

I turned to Buckner and tersely instructed him to stand fast. Without waiting around for an acknowledgement from either party I spurred forward, away from the expectant group. A familiar knot of tension had developed in my stomach. My mouth was suddenly parched.

The trail, such as it was, drifted off to the right, behind a large outcrop of rock. Disregarding all natural caution, I galloped out of sight of the others. For some reason I had not even drawn a weapon. Intuitively, I knew that I would not be under threat.

The sight that I beheld caused me to jerk back savagely on the reins, so as to have me almost out of the saddle. Before me was the delectable figure of Ana de Luna, as I had never expected to see her.

Two stout pieces of pecan timber had been roped together to form a letter X and then propped up against a huge boulder. Ana's wrists and ankles were strapped to the frame, so forcing her body to replicate its shape. Her entire upper body was naked to the world. The vestiges of her blouse hung in tatters around her arms. Her full, perfectly proportioned breasts were displayed for all to see.

Reluctantly I tore my gaze from them and swiftly scanned the rest of her form. A length of cloth was tied around her neck, tightly enough to severely restrict her breathing and curtail all speech. As if all of that wasn't bad enough, a series of cuts had been made in her trousers, sufficiently deep to draw blood.

Although shocked, I was still sufficiently compos mentis to realize that what I witnessed was actually a display. Its sole intention was to provoke a reaction.

If I were to counter that reaction I would have to move fast, yet a combination of lust and pity seemed to rob me of the ability to move. As my gaze came to rest on her face, her eyes met mine. Desperately she strained to utter a plea, but no words came. My heart urged me to bound forward and cut her free, but my head made me wheel about and gallop back to the others.

As I approached the bend in the trail I encountered Kirby and Buckner.

'Where's Lee?' I demanded before they had any chance to speak.

Kirby eyed me speculatively as he replied:

'Down the trail a ways, keeping Santa Anna company.'

'Make sure they stay there. Tell them that Buckner spotted skirmishers in the hills and we need to make sure it's safe to continue. Then come on after me – and hurry!'

Having no doubt heard of the point man's discovery, the sergeant knew better than to argue. Satisfied, I wheeled my horse around yet again and returned to Ana. I moved slowly, searching the broken terrain for Tylee's position. I knew that he had to be close enough to both hold a gun on her and maintain a dialogue with me.

As I approached the pathetic hostage she struggled vainly against the unyielding restraints. The effort caused her breasts to heave in a most seductive fashion. Her eyes were locked on mine, as though she was attempting to transmit a message. It occurred to me that she very probably knew where the lieutenant was.

I withdrew a Colt Walker from the right saddle holster and carefully dismounted. I could not risk using the scatter-gun.

Again I longed to rush forward and cut her loose, but I knew that would result in my death and probably hers as well. Ana's glance abruptly shifted beyond me, signifying the arrival of Kirby and his rangers. For them her appearance was just too much to take in without comment.

'The little lady's trussed up like a chicken!'

'Yeah and *what* a chicken. Damn, but I'd like to—'

Anger flared up within me and Ranger Seward never got a chance to elaborate. 'You men will remember why we are here. Any—'

What I was about to say was cut off by a familiar voice, emanating from the rocks behind Ana.

'You took your sweet time getting here, Major Collins, sir.'

'Damn your insolence and damn you!' I bellowed back instinctively.

A few yards away, amongst a jumble of rocks, Tylee's face appeared, just behind the gaping muzzle of a purloined Colt Walker. It was aimed unwaveringly at his helpless captive.

'Any more talk like that and I'll place a ball in her delightful body.'

'If you harm her I'll shoot you myself, or see you hanged at General Scott's convenience.'

'Yeah, but you won't let it happen, will you? I've seen the way you look at her. You'd like to show her some English hospitality, ha-ha. Besides, I haven't come all this way just to molest some pampered bitch. It's her papa that I want.'

I resisted the impulse to take issue with him. We both knew he had the advantage.

'So here's the deal,' he continued. 'You give me a clear shot at Santa Anna and she goes free. Once he's dead your mission will be over. You'll be able to return to Veracruz and I'll just up and disappear. You can blame it all on me.'

'You know I can't do that,' I replied hotly.

'Why not?' he flung back. 'President Polk's the only one that'll be riled and he's in Washington.'

The conversation was getting us nowhere, a fact that was highlighted by Kirby's next observation:

'Looks like we got us a real Mexican stand-off, Major.'

I stood there, my huge revolver hanging impotently at my right side, and glumly contemplated the options available to me. Tylee had the tactical sense to remain silent. I was between a rock and a hard place. A swift glance around the assembled rangers gave me no comfort. To a man, they were all greedily drinking in Ana's enforced provocative posture. The lieutenant obviously possessed a high level of innate cunning. By bringing lust and sexual domination into the equation, he had made it all the harder for me to give her up in favour of her father. In addition, by unsettling and arousing me he had hampered my ability to make any considered decision.

Only Kirby managed to contribute anything constructive, but even that had a sour note to it.

'You're gonna have to leave her to the buzzards, else those seven rangers died for nothing.'

Sweat flowed freely over me as tension built up within my body. The burden of command had never been heavier. I had absolutely no idea what to do and the knowledge tormented me. But for the *señora's* lack of clothing, all eyes would surely have been on me.

There was an ominous click, sufficient to penetrate my desperate musings. Tylee had retracted the hammer to full cock. It was obviously partly a theatrical gesture, designed to increase the pressure on me. It put me on notice that the mere contraction of his right forefinger was sufficient to send a .44-calibre ball into Ana's totally exposed body. At that range such a projectile would undoubtedly be lethal.

God help me! What should I do?

The pounding of hoofs on parched earth resounded behind me. I turned in surprise to observe Santa Anna galloping hell for leather towards us. Behind him, in belated pursuit, came Robert Lee. As the manic horseman closed on us I realized that he would stop for no man. His face was suffused with rage. In his right hand he brandished the pepperbox that had proved so temperamental on the beach.

'*Yanqui bastardo,*' he howled.

'Move it, boys,' yelled Kirby superfluously. 'He'll tump us all.'

Abruptly relieved of my appalling dilemma, I now knew exactly what was needed. Everything hinged on Tylee's reaction. He had demanded a clear shot at Santa Anna; yet finding his intended victim charging directly at him with a loaded gun was something else again. I cocked my own piece and waited for his inevitable reaction. As Santa Anna swept past me Tylee swung his revolver over to face the threat.

I unsheathed my knife and bounded forward. At the same moment Tylee's gun discharged. The heavy ball caught Santa Anna in the left leg. The brutal impact forced his upper body to pivot forward in the saddle before pitching him bodily off the horse. The rangers had, to a man, also dropped to the ground. Instinctively, I knew that they would be reluctant to engage in a firefight with their fellow countryman. To them it seemed that he had a genuine grievance, which excused his present conduct.

Tylee fired again, leaving me in no doubt that I would have to take him on by myself. I reached Ana and sliced through her bonds.

'Flee for your life!' I yelled, of necessity ignoring her cries of distress.

I turned back to face my foe. I now found him lining up his weapon on me. I took rapid aim and squeezed the trigger. With an encouraging crash the Colt discharged, yet the very speed of my action told against me and the ball went wide. Wreathed in black powder smoke, I leapt to one side just in time. Tylee, unsettled by my fire, also misjudged his shot, which was often the way of things.

I drew in a deep breath and, using both hands to support my weapon, I took deliberate aim. This time there was no doubt over the outcome. The heavy projectile struck the naval officer full in the chest. Slammed back into a boulder, he stayed almost upright, disbelief etched across his ruddy face. With a fresh cap under the hammer, I cautiously advanced. His eyes took in the muzzle pointed at his skull, but there was a total absence of fear. He was too far gone for that. Blood frothed out over his moustache and down his chin; gradually he slid sideways and then down to the ground. As I eased the revolver from his feeble grasp he made a supreme effort to focus on me. I had to strain to hear his last words.

'You done killed me, English, but I'll haunt your remaining days. God damn y—'

Exhaling blood, his head lolled on his chest and he was gone.

I returned to the others with decidedly mixed feelings. I had just taken the life of a brave man, whose only crime was that of attempting to avenge his brother's death. Yet he had left me with no choice.

My self-recrimination ended abruptly at the sight of Santa Anna being hauled none too gently to his feet by Kirby and Lee. Convinced that that was no way to treat any wounded man, I called out for them to desist.

'Just winded is all, Major,' Kirby replied, regarding me with genuine amusement.

'That cannot be,' I responded heatedly. 'I saw him take a ball.'

'In the *left* leg, Major Collins,' stated Robert Lee with gentle insistence.

The general had at last got his breath.

'*Sí, sí.* They speak the truth.' He then proceeded to stamp the earth with that very limb: the wood and cork limb. It was eerie, observing the rent in his trousers, to realize that he was completely unharmed.

'Yet again I owe you a great debt, *señor.* Whatever you think of me as an *hombre*, you must not doubt my love for my dearest Ana. She means much to me.'

At the mention of his daughter I turned eagerly to search her out. For in truth, given the extreme situation, I had temporarily forgotten all about her. To my surprise, I spotted her huddled in a blanket, some distance from the others.

You oaf! I chided myself. She was hardly likely to be seeking comfort with the rangers. Their only interest in her was of a base, carnal nature. I too had such thoughts, but I preferred to think that they were of a more refined variety.

Still clutching two enormous handguns, I made my way over to her. As I approached she sprang to her feet and appeared to be about to fling herself at me. Yet something in my manner must have restrained her, because instead she merely beamed up at me. Her face was grubby and tearstained, yet still her beauty shone through.

'You saved me from that – that – *cerdo*. After all that I said to you, you still saved me.'

Although conscious that I had not actually done anything to release her, other than slice through the cords, it felt grand to be the recipient of such adoration. Such was her excitement that the edges of the blanket slipped from her grasp and I received an enticingly visible reward. Although aware of her effect on me, Ana made no attempt to conceal her breasts. Had we been alone, our relationship could possibly have taken a delightful turn, but of course it was not to be.

Conscious of many pairs of eyes on us, I gently rearranged the material around her.

'The time is not right,' I murmured softly. 'You are not among friends. Please find something to wear. If you do not have anything, then I will see what can be done.'

'Do not concern yourself,' she replied, nodding gravely. 'I have something in my bags. I will take myself off to bathe these cuts. *Ese maldito hombre*, why would he do such things to me?'

From behind me there came the sound of steady footfalls. Turning round, I found myself facing the grave figure of Captain Robert Lee.

'You must pardon this intrusion, sir,' he said, courteous as ever. Then, waiting until Ana had moved out of earshot, he continued: 'I felt that you should be aware that there is ill feeling against you amongst some of the rank and file.'

'What, in particular, are they unhappy with now, pray?' I enquired, gazing at him quizzically.

Lee appeared genuinely surprised.

'You are burdened with a great deal of responsibility, but surely it cannot have escaped your notice that you have just killed a serving officer of the United States Navy?'

CHAPTER SEVEN

The dark looks and muttered threats came to nothing, but if ever it could be said that mutiny was in the air then I had smelt it. That nothing came to pass was down to the respect that they held for Sergeant Kirby and his forceful reminder of what would await them if they did not heed Colonel Hays's original instructions. In truth it was only two or three of the men, including Buckner and Seward, who had forcefully expressed dissatisfaction with my actions.

Going on the assumption that hard work silences dissident tongues, I instructed them to bury the lieutenant at a depth sufficient to discourage scavengers. A rough marker was whittled out and Lee did his best to record the site for any of his family who might wish to see it.

Our ranks had now been reduced from one score to one dozen.

That night, as I lay enveloped in the single blanket necessary to ward off the night's chill, I was suddenly roused out of a deep sleep by a truly piercing scream. I jerked upright and instinctively reached out for my Paterson Colt. I had retained it on my person since it was a smaller, more manageable weapon. From off to my left came the sounds of a scuffle. I got myself unsteadily to my feet and stumbled over there. I knew

96

instinctively that Ana would be involved and so it proved.

I caught a vivid picture of her under the pale moonlight, standing bolt upright. Her clothes were in disarray and she was trembling uncontrollably. Buckner was lying at her feet, blood pouring from a deep cut in his left cheek. For an instant I thought that she was responsible, having acted to defend her honour. Then I caught sight of the blade in Kirby's right hand, and everything became clear.

'You just don't get it, do you?' he snarled. 'Whatever you think on these greasers, they're the reason we're all here. We're under orders.'

The sergeant paused as he gazed around at the startled rangers. Even Santa Anna, still resplendent in his uniform despite the ungodly hour, held his peace. Any indignation that he may have felt at being referred to as a 'greaser' was kept well hidden. He contented himself with comforting his daughter. Glancing down at the stricken ranger, Kirby continued:

'Reckon you're gonna need some stitching. All of you think on that next time you fancy poking the lady.'

His emphasis on the last word left his opinion of her open to debate, but not so the rest of his words. The other rangers warily backed away from him before returning to their bedrolls. Ignoring Buckner, who was dabbing tentatively at his damaged flesh, I approached the two Mexicans. Ana's eyes were like glistening pools in the silvery light.

'I must apologize for this ruffian's conduct,' I said, bowing slightly, 'but as you can plainly see it will not be tolerated.'

The wayward ranger muttered something unintelligible as he shuffled away. Ignoring him, as he would any common soldier, the general returned my gesture of courtesy.

'Such behaviour is commonplace in any army, mine included.'

I could not pass up such an opportunity.

'Surely it's not your army until your president places it under your command?'

Santa Anna's eyes seemed to glitter as he regarded me.

'A mere formality,' he replied smoothly. 'The war goes badly for Farias, *sí*? He has *yanquis* on his very doorstep. He needs a man of . . . how shall I say? *Sí, sí* . . . of my experience.'

Before I could comment further he gave an exaggerated yawn and placed his arm protectively around his daughter.

'It is late, Major Collins,' he remarked with an air of finality. 'We should continue this another time. *Buenas noches.*'

Slowly I turned away, and returned to my blanket. Was it my imagination, or was there a sharper chill in the air? Perhaps our ever-increasing height above sea level was to blame. Or perhaps His Excellency had that effect on everybody.

The arrival of my fourth day in Mexico heralded another problem of our own making.

Sergeant Kirby was all for moving on, but it was obvious to me that Buckner's open wound needed attention. He would be of little use to us if it became infected. Accordingly I asked for a volunteer to wield a needle. Surprisingly, it was Davey Jackson who stepped forward. I had expected one of Buckner's particular cronies, but then Jackson himself was no longer a callow youth. Also, some of the old hands appeared to be influenced by Kirby's disdain for the whole procedure. To him, Buckner had brought all this on himself and was now causing us to waste daylight.

To give him his due, the errant ranger remained stubbornly silent throughout the whole process. As the sharp point penetrated his tender flesh the man just clenched his fists and ground his teeth. Fresh blood trickled from his face and seeped into his buckskins. Even when his friend Seward poured some 'bug juice' over the injury to ward off infection he still retained his composure.

I was impressed, but Kirby was having none of it.

'If you ladies have done finished with your knitting, we got us some ground to cover.'

The road to Perote twisted like a snake through the hills. As we moved ever higher, it was hard to believe that we were still in the tropics. A low mist seemed to have enveloped us and the sweat generated by all movement was a thing of the past. One thing was for sure, whatever might have been the situation on the coast, up there we were entirely free of disease.

Our progress throughout that long day was slow. On two occasions we had to pull off the trail to avoid armed columns heading east. Scott's invasion had thrown the country into turmoil.

At last, with the onset of evening, the town came into view. Or rather one particular structure did. The huge stone fortress of San Carlos dominated the town and its environs. Square, with sheer walls and surrounded by a large moat, it possessed a stark, brutal aura. Whoever held that citadel, held Perote.

Lying beside me on a prominent rock, Robert Lee scrutinized our destination through his spyglass. The rest of my command was cold-camped below us, well away from the highway.

'Very impressive,' he commented drily. 'Do I take it that we won't be advancing in column of twos, with flags unfurled?'

'Ha! Well . . . that might be His Excellency's wish. Who knows?' I replied with a smile. 'But what I know is that a repeat of our victory in Xalapa would finish us. Yet we do badly need some intelligence.'

Affected by anxiety, my comment must have carried further than intended, because Ana called up from below:

'I will find out what you require.'

Cursing my careless tongue, I scrambled over the smooth rock and dropped down next to her. As was usual in her presence, my heart pumped that little bit faster. I longed to reach out and touch her, but had to content myself with a purely vocal response.

'I cannot allow that. Such an undertaking would carry too much risk.'

Ignoring the slack-jawed spectators, she flashed a most brilliant smile.

'Do not concern yourself, Major Collins. I can pass as a simple *peon*, merely returning to *mi casa*.'

I regarded her askance. 'You don't look anything like a *peon*, simple or otherwise.'

'A horse-blanket and some mud is all I require. I have the language and . . . how you say . . . the look that none of you gringos possesses.'

Santa Anna placed a gloved hand on my right forearm, as though to still any further objections.

'Of course she must go. We – both of us – must know who holds the town.'

He was perfectly correct, of course, but that fact didn't alter the waspishness of my response.

'My concern is for her safety, which you have obviously taken into account.'

With that, I tore my arm from his grasp and took another of my fateful decisions. 'Very well, go. But for God's sake, be careful. Any danger, get out of there fast!'

I turned to Kirby. 'You heard the lady, Sergeant. A blanket and some mud.'

As usual that man had the last word.

'Oh, she'll get a blanket all right, but I can't vouch for the ticks in it.'

It was fully dark when Ana returned, breathless from both the

100

altitude and excitement, but fairly bubbling with enthusiasm.

'The town is full of *soldados*. General Ampudia has arrived with many guns. *Muy grande.*'

'Ampudia, here?' Santa Anna clapped his hands together in delight. 'He will follow me. He is a *conservador*. I can arrive in Mexico City with an army behind me.'

That ill-guarded remark confirmed what I had always suspected about His Excellency's plans. He did not intend to offer his services to President Farias; he was out to depose him. All of which was acceptable enough, of course, if he then stuck to his agreement with the United States government.

Still flushed with triumph, Ana was eager to retain her audience. That led her to relate something that, in the interests of her country, she should have kept to herself.

'There are prisoners in the fortress. American *soldados*, captured at Monterrey.'

'Monterrey?' The whole damnable business was coming full circle. Even the Mexican general in command there had turned up like a bad penny.

Santa Anna, his face suddenly like thunder, tried to brush such matters aside.

'Pah! Common soldiers held prisoner. It is a risk of making war and of no interest to me.'

Kirby placed himself nose to nose with the general.

'Well, it's of interest to me, your highness. If you've got some of our boys in that there fort, then it's odds on some of them'll be Texicans. And I ain't leaving no Texican to rot in any Mex jail.'

The two men eyeballed each other for some time; eventually Santa Anna looked away. He was undoubtedly a brave man, but he knew only too well that in such company he stood little chance.

With a sinking feeling I realized that I now had another problem to contend with. Captain Robert E. Lee summed the situation up concisely.

'If I may comment, Major? When His Excellency here makes contact with General Ampudia our task is over. We are free to return to the coast, mission accomplished. If, however, we attempt to release the prisoners, then everything changes. We could not possibly allow him to join his compatriots in case he forestalls us. Which, of course, would be in direct contravention of the orders given to you.'

I was in equal measure impressed and depressed.

'Captain Lee, you have made a capital job of articulating my dilemma. However, it is for me – and me alone – to choose a course of action.'

Unfortunately, Sergeant Kirby saw it slightly differently.

'You can choose away, Major, but I ain't hightailing it back to Veracruz and leaving our men behind.'

There was muttered support from the other rangers clustered around us in the gloom. Damn it all! Why couldn't Ana have kept her pretty mouth shut? Vainly I tried to protest.

'What if there are no rangers held there? Then what?'

Kirby favoured me with a look that spoke volumes.

'You was there, Thomas. We were in the thick of it and lost some good boys. But maybe they're not all dead. You won't likely know this, but when the Santa Fe expedition of '41 got itself bushwhacked by the Mexes, many Texicans ended up in that cursed fortress. They were left to rot for over a year. That ain't gonna happen this time.'

There was an ominous air of finality to his little speech, along with open backing from his men. It appeared that this time I had a definite mutiny on my hands, but one that I could hardly condemn. What Kirby said next sealed the matter for me.

'Lead us, or leave us. I couldn't give a shit either way!' As he uttered that dismissive remark he softened it with a wink of one eye that was meant for me alone.

Since it was apparent that I wasn't entirely friendless I went on the offensive.

'Have any of you men ever assaulted a fortress without artillery support?'

The answer was, of course, in the negative. Comanche raiding parties never defended structures of any kind.

'Well then, I will lead you, but you will follow my instructions to the letter. And one of you will have to stand guard over General Santa Anna.' There were cries of protest, but I talked over them. 'Whether this crazy attempt succeeds or not, whoever stays here eventually allows the general to join his people.'

I peered through the gloom at the assembled group, steeling myself for trouble.

'Makes no odds to me,' Kirby stated softly. 'We'll either be heading full chisel for the coast, or we'll be dead.'

There were a few chuckles. The mood noticeably lightened, until Mexico's former ruler spoke out again.

'You would dare make me your prisoner?' he hissed.

'I have no choice,' I responded. 'If you joined Ampudia now you could hardly stand by whilst we attacked his garrison.' Allowing him no time to reply, I pressed on fast. 'I will leave it up to you, Sergeant, to decide who stays. My interest now is with the fortress.'

Then, attempting to sound far more confident than I actually felt, I quietly addressed them all.

'We are going to rescue your countrymen and I know how it is to be done.'

Suddenly I had their full attention. 'Nine of us cannot hope to force that stronghold, so instead we are going to just walk right in. And Señora de Luna is the key to everything.'

Robert Lee was regarding me with interest, but he remained silent. Not so Sergeant Kirby.

'Just walk right in,' he echoed sarcastically, executing a flat sweeping arc with his right hand. 'Without so much as a "by your leave"?'

Ignoring him, I doggedly continued: 'On the authority of General Ampudia, Señora de Luna will demand entry for herself and her escort. Which, since we will be that escort, is another reason to do this under cover of darkness. She is charged with inspecting the Yankee prisoners, to discover if there are certain Mexican deserters amongst them who once laboured on her family's demesne.

'It is pure fabrication, but should serve to get her – us – inside. Once there, we will release everyone we find and break out again. Some use of force will perhaps be necessary.' Which was, quite possibly, the understatement of the year.

No one uttered a word. The sheer audacity of my plan appeared to have taken everyone's breath away. I turned to Ana.

'Are you prepared to help us?' I asked softly. Her reply was swift.

'I will help *you, sí*.'

'*Gracias, señora*,' I returned. 'In that case I need you to appear as aristocratic as possible. The guards must be in awe of your position. Do you have anything in your bags similar to that which you wore on the Mississippi?'

She smiled knowingly. 'I did not leave everything on the ship. I will see what I can do.'

She turned away and faded into the gloom. Santa Anna's eyes seemed to burn like hot coals as he watched her depart.

'General, you will remain here with Davey Jackson. Whatever occurs in that fortress, whether we succeed or fail, you with be released tomorrow, unharmed.'

That gave him the chance to vent some of his undoubted indignation on to me.

'I must protest, Major! I am not your prisoner.'

'No, but you are temporarily under my command and you

will do as I say.'

Before he had time to reply Davey intervened.

'You need all the men that you can get, Major. Whyn't we just tie him up and leave him?'

'Yeah,' added Seward. 'Truss him up like a chicken.'

'Enough,' I barked. The proceedings were beginning to resemble a town meeting. 'My orders were that the general should be delivered to his compatriots. Leaving him tied to a tree does not fulfil that requirement. Davey, I can trust you to see that no harm comes to him.'

That was more a statement than a question, but nevertheless I stopped and stared at the young ranger. If it had been daylight I would probably have witnessed colour rising in his face. He swallowed.

'Don't worry, Major,' he replied, 'you can rely on me.'

'I know. That's why your sergeant recommended you.' Smiling at the sudden expression of satisfaction on his young face, I added: 'Once you have released the general you will have to use your own initiative. Try to link up with us. If not . . . well you'll just have to make your own way back to Xalapa.'

I turned to the others. Santa Anna had now become noticeably withdrawn, as though he was no longer part of the situation. If I had been less preoccupied I might have recognized the danger signs. As it was I moved straight on to our preparations for the coming ordeal. In spite of my confident delivery I was under no illusions about what lay ahead. Robert Lee's considered remark best summed up the problem facing us.

'We don't look any thing like Mexican conscripts, sir.'

'I agree, but I'm hoping that the guards will be so taken aback by Ana's finery and your own good self in His Excellency's tunic that they won't scrutinize the rest of us lurking in the background.'

Now that did get a response. Whilst the captain looked

merely amused by the idea, the 'Napoleon of the West' appeared to be on the point of apoplexy. I forestalled his expected protests with a well-reasoned threat.

'My request is non-negotiable, General. Your tunic may well assist your daughter in her subterfuge and so improve our chances. Please remove it, or I will ask for volunteers to assist you.'

With a face like thunder, slowly and grudgingly he unbuttoned and removed his tunic.

Only as we resumed our advance on Perote, now on foot, did I realize just how tired I was – and there would be no sleep for any of us that night. Just how any of the men whom we released were to get away was, of course, another problem. As I had no idea of their numbers or condition we were very much taking a leap of faith.

Ana had effected a remarkable transformation. Gone was the overtly male attire, to be replaced by a flowing cream skirt; all frills and lace, along with an intricately embroidered blouse. Somehow she had managed to clean her face and the overall result was amazing. By her side marched Captain Lee, resplendent in his borrowed – and hastily brushed-up – uniform tunic. I was confident that no lowly Mexican conscript could possibly resist their combined splendour.

As I followed in their wake I could sense the reinvigorated mood of the men around me. With Davey languishing back in camp, Kirby now had six rangers under his command. For the first time in the mission those men felt that they had a task worthy of their talents. Nursemaiding a hated warlord had never been to their taste. Every man had his rifle slung over his back and was clutching at least one fully charged Colt Walker. If all went well the weapons would remain unfired.

At last the fortress prison of San Carlos came into view. Just beyond its huge walls lay the town of Perote, rather like a mediaeval village nestling under the parapet of the lord's castle. Having kept away from the main track I instructed my little band to gather round. In hushed tones I issued my final orders.

'All revolvers in your belts, behind your backs. No eye contact with any of the guards. And don't get too close to Ana and the captain. They must be the focus of attention.'

Every man's eyes were on me. Never had they accorded me such rapt attention. The men were about to do what they had all signed up for: fight Mexicans! There was only one thing left to be said:

'May your God go with you and good luck to us all!'

Catching sight of Ana's strained features, I realized that she must be very nervous; suspicion entered my mind. How could she not feel a sense of guilt at conniving with us against her own people? Or was she about to turn the tables on us?

Then we were on the move again, and there was no time for doubts or fears. Ana and Lee stepped out on to the main thoroughfare and their whole deportment abruptly changed. Their pace slowed to that of a languid stroll. Elegantly clad shoulders were straightened up. Their heads were held high, thereby allowing them to view the world imperiously from a new standpoint. Without observing their faces, I could still almost feel the arrogance flowing from them. Conversely, the remainder of us had, with little prompting necessary, adopted the careless slouch of poorly paid conscripts for whom life held no prospects.

The track soon brought us level with the moat. A short distance ahead was a right turn leading to the causeway that traversed it. Once on that there was no turning back. I glanced briefly over at Kirby's grim features. Catching my eye, he shrugged his shoulders and remained silent. There really was nothing left to say.

CHAPTER EIGHT

As we turned on to the causeway the flickering lamplight played over us. Hardly daring to breathe, I awaited the inevitable peremptory challenge. With alarming speed the forbidding walls drew closer. Still there was no reaction to our advance. If I was affected by the tension, then what state could Ana be in?

Before us loomed an arched gateway through the outer walls. I became aware of an unpleasant stench assailing my nostrils. As we had been in open country for some days the odour of unwashed bodies and excreta came as an unwelcome surprise. Under the wide brim of my hat my gaze roamed everywhere. Then I saw him. A startled face had appeared at a crenellation in the parapet. Instantly its owner shouted down to his comrades in the gatehouse. Our time had arrived.

A sergeant and three privates shambled out of a guardroom. They sported dark-blue coats and trousers, the former decorated with yellow braid and the latter with a red stripe. On their heads perched blue stovepipe shakos, decorated with a red ball plume at the front. They appeared to be a throwback to the Napoleonic era, but there was no doubting the deadliness of the bayonets atop their smoothbore muskets. These were men of the Mexican foot artillery under the direct command of General Pedro de Ampudia.

108

All four of them had the hard-bitten look of seasoned regulars, but even the non-commissioned officer was temporarily lost for words. As he took in the glorious vision of Ana de Luna his jaw worked, but no sound was forthcoming. Surrounded by all the accoutrements of war and oppression, he could never have expected to encounter such an enchanting member of the female sex. That was her moment and she seized it.

'*Me llamo Ana Leticia Arellano de Luna.*'

I understood no more after that, other than frequent references to General Ampudia and *soldados yanquis*. Again doubt reared its ugly head. Was she referring to the supposed prisoners or us? The splendidly attired Robert Lee nodded gravely from time to time, but otherwise remained necessarily silent. The success of the whole ploy rested solely on Ana's slight shoulders. Whilst she did not deign to smile at a mere lowly sergeant it soon became clear that her intoxicating presence was having its effect. The man's head began to nod with increasing vigour, whilst his saucer-like eyes had taken on an almost childlike appearance. Then, to my intense relief, he handed his musket to a subordinate and spread his arms in supplication. With barely a glance at the rest of us, he turned to lead her into his inner sanctum. We were in.

Once through the rectangular gatehouse we found ourselves in a large enclosed courtyard. The surrounding walls were ringed with flickering lamps and I felt frighteningly exposed. A platoon of infantry, stationed on the walkways, could have finished us in seconds. Yet there was no one in sight.

It eventually dawned on me that the fortress of San Carlos was, at that moment, more of a prison than a defensive structure. The guards were only there to supervise the inmates. General Scott was still too far away to represent a serious threat.

Feeling almost light-headed, I watched as the artillery sergeant motioned obsequiously for her ladyship to follow him down a flight of steps. As her 'escort' brought up the rear over the worn uneven slabs, I marvelled that no one had objected to our entry into the citadel's inner sanctum. Apparently no officer deigned to serve as jailer during the hours of darkness and the non-commissioned subordinate was completely bewitched by the *señora*.

A wide arched corridor led to another set of stone steps. The walls were coated with slime, the dampness was almost tangible. For the first time it occurred to me that any prisoners held down there might not be in any condition to flee at speed. We really had no idea what we were getting ourselves into.

At last we arrived in what could only be described as a dungeon. Leading off it was a number of heavily barred wooden doors with latticed grilles at chest height.

The sergeant had joined another three guards, but they were of a completely different calibre from those in the gatehouse. These men were unkempt and dishevelled, clad in filthy uniforms and barely recognizable as soldiers. Like their *compadres* above, they were all *mestizos*: Mexican-Indian half-castes, but of a distinctly poorer quality.

As we all filed into the chamber a range of emotions registered on their foul, dissipated faces. Confronted by Ana in all her finery, they immediately displayed unbridled lust. Their beady eyes crawled all over her, mentally striping her of both clothes and dignity. Then, as the room filled with heavily armed men, other emotions came to the fore. Nervous uncertainty replaced desire and they began to peer longingly at their weapons, which lay strewn around just out of reach.

Something in their expressions communicated itself to the sergeant, causing him to blink rapidly as he assessed us, seemingly for the first time, in the flickering light. His jaw tightened as he took in both our weapons and general appearance. There came a burst of rapid Spanish as he questioned Ana in a far less deferential tone. She in turn remained composed and replied in the manner of a true member of the Mexican nobility. I had no real hope of understanding any of it, although I did catch a few words that hinted at her explanation. The use of *vaqueros* and *mi hacienda*, suggested that she was attempting to pass us off as her personal retainers.

Whilst this was taking place something else developed that was soon to render it all irrelevant. I became aware that one of the jailers was staring fixedly at Rance Buckner. The livid scar on that man's cheek, which no amount of facial hair could conceal, seemed to be a source of fascination to the simple fool. The ranger became aware of the unwelcome attention and returned the stare, but whereas the *mestizo*'s eyes displayed the curiosity of an almost retarded sensibility, Buckner's conveyed a savage hostility. He nudged Seward and together they began to edge forward.

I could see where this was leading, but to reprimand Buckner would have completely given the game away. Silently cursing, I allowed my right hand to drift towards the smaller, less noticeable Paterson Colt tucked in my trousers' front. Although a blade would have made more sense, knife-fighting rarely came naturally to a British officer.

With a dreadful sense of foreboding I somehow managed to observe both scenarios simultaneously. To my left, Ana seemed finally to have convinced the sergeant of her patriotic intentions. To my right, the simple peon was unwittingly facing a bloody death. His fellows, noticing the ominous advance of Buckner and Seward, belatedly reached for their Brown Bess muskets.

That was all the provocation the rangers needed. With the rapidity of a striking snake Buckner leapt forward. Employing

111

ferocious force, he plunged his knife into the simpleton's throat. Such was the width of the blade that he almost severed the man's head. Blood cascaded over his filthy attire and he died without a sound.

His two companions had seized their weapons and were frantically cocking the hammers. The sudden violence had taken the other rangers by surprise. They had been too engrossed in Ana's subtle entreaties. Because of the swiftness of his victim's swift collapse Buckner could not immediately free his knife and he was blocking Seward's path.

With practised speed I drew and cocked my revolver. Muskets are cumbersome at close quarters and the guards had to choose between many targets. I only had two.

Pointing my piece at the nearest torso, I squeezed the trigger. In such a confined space the detonation was horrendous. The agonized scream that followed was nearly as deafening. With a cloud of sulphurous smoke impeding my view, I instinctively swung to the left, thumbing back the hammer as I did so. Again I fired, bringing pain lancing into my eardrums. A couple of anguished cries followed, one from directly in front of me and another from the far end of the chamber. As of habit I again readied my Colt, but as the smoke dissipated it was obvious that I would not require the next chamber. Of the two luckless turnkeys, one had taken a ball square in the chest and was clearly dead. The other had taken his round only in the left shoulder, but was being viciously bludgeoned to death by his own musket in the hands of Ranger Seward.

I turned away from the gore and rushed over to Ana's side. The sergeant whom she had bewitched was lying curled up before her, drenched in blood. Kirby, who had obviously stabbed him repeatedly in the belly, was in the act of disengaging his knife. Ana, still not yet accustomed to sudden bursts of bloody violence, was trembling uncontrollably.

Conscious of our parlous situation, I singled out one of the other rangers.

'See if anyone above heard all this. Go carefully.'

Kirby got to his feet.

'You's like to blow my eardrums with all that shooting,' he commented laconically,

As there was a perpetual ringing in my right ear his words sounded strangely disjointed. Before I could respond, though, there came a remarkable interruption from beyond one of the locked doors.

'Sweet Jesus, you be Texicans!'

This was followed swiftly by: 'Open this goddamned door!'

For a brief moment there was a stunned silence. Then suddenly everyone's face held a smile.

'Search them greasers for keys, boys,' bellowed Kirby.

The ranger whom I had sent off to reconnoitre returned to infom us that thick walls and two flights of stairs had muffled our dark deeds. Simultaneously, Seward discovered the keys and his comrades clustered round the first door.

Robert Lee, appearing strangely incongruous in his gaudy uniform, manoeuvred me away from the mêlée. With my ear still ringing, I had to strain to hear his words.

'When that sergeant does not reappear they will come looking. With your permission I would know your plans, just in case you have overlooked something, sir.'

Always calm and collected, Lee was thinking ahead. As the heavy key turned in the lock I responded:

'My stratagem is to free and arm any whom we find and then break out while it's still dark. We return to Davey, send Santa Anna on his way and then flee with all speed. Of course it all turns on whom we find in these cells.'

As he digested that intelligence the cell door creaked open. Even standing at some remove we were assailed by an overpowering stench. Ana gagged and fled for the stairs whilst even the enthusiastic rangers held back. From out of the dark, fetid room a wildly bearded fellow emerged, clutching a buckskin bag. This apparition blinked repeatedly in the lamp-light. Such was his appearance that we all fell silent and remained quite still.

Gradually, as he became accustomed to the light, he peered at each of us in turn. As he did so some form of real-ization appeared to come over him. Tears began to well up in his eyes, until soon the liquid was coursing unchecked down his cheeks. Even to hardened frontiersmen and soldiers like us it was a pitiable sight. My natural inclination was to offer him some comfort, but I took my lead from Kirby and his rangers. They were his countrymen and their ways were not always mine.

There was movement in the cell behind him and other equally unkempt characters began hesitantly to appear. Physically they seemed quite unmatched to the strong voices we had heard only minutes before. The reality of being released had obviously taxed them sorely.

As the man before us caught sight of the stricken artillery sergeant he effected a remarkable transformation. Sheer hatred twisted his features and he kicked out viciously at the man's face. For some moments no one had the temerity to stop him. He had quite obviously been badly used by the soldier and there was no harm in allowing him to work out his pent-up loathing on a corpse. Eventually Kirby gripped him firmly by the shoulders.

'Save it, fella. There's plenty of live ones up them stairs.'

The other man froze in his grip, as though unused to friendly contact with another human being. Only gradually did the manic look in his eyes dissipate. Then finally he nodded his acquiescence.

Slowly but surely his comrades joined him in the chamber. They too were disoriented but, encouragingly, were all able to walk unaided. Some glanced briefly at the pulverized Mexican sergeant, but none displayed any overt hostility, possibly because his features were, by then, all but unrecognizable. There appeared to be roughly a score of men delivered from captivity. However, if they were to remain free, certain decisions had to be taken.

I backed off on to the stairs so as to distance myself from the others and peremptorily summoned Kirby. My instructions were as follows;

'Ascertain the physical capabilities of all the rescued men. Discover whether they have any knowledge that would assist in our escape. Distribute the dead guards' weapons to the most able of those rescued.'

The ranger sergeant listened attentively, then departed without demur to do my bidding. Suddenly I was overcome with weariness and I dropped down on to a worn step. I was aware that Ana was also taking her ease a little further up the stairs. I felt that I ought to congratulate her on her fine performance, but I was just too tired. I called out for Lee to rejoin me, then commenced the laborious task of reloading the two discharged chambers of my revolver.

'Captain, those artillery *soldados* will be missing their sergeant soon. We must make our move. In your opinion, can we make it to Veracruz with so many enfeebled men? Remember, we have spare horses for less than half their number.'

Lee's facial expression was lost on me, for I was forcing a slightly oversized lead ball into a powder chamber, but I absorbed every word of his reply.

'I believe that you must take either all or none, because to draw lots would be altogether too cruel after what they have gone through. And, of course, we did come here to rescue them. I also believe that by the time we reach Xalapa we shall find American forces there. I know General Scott. He will not long remain at the coast. The threat of *vomito* will be ever on his mind.' With that he fell silent.

As ever, his comments had been concise and well considered and they had confirmed my own course of action. Having replaced the spent percussion caps, I stuffed the revolver into my belt and reached behind me for the Colt Walker. If there were to be action, then that weapon would serve me better.

So far I had avoided all direct contact with the foul-smelling additions to our forces. I was aware that some of them were regarding me curiously, but the requirement for swift action precluded the luxury of my making their acquaintance. I rejoined Kirby and enquired as to his findings.

'They're all dead beat, but they'll follow you out of here if they have to crawl. Them other cells are all empty. The greasers piled them into one to save time. Seven are Texicans, the rest hail from any state you can think of. And they're all a mite rank.'

'In that case the night air will do them good,' I replied caustically. I suddenly knew what needed to be done and I was anxious to be about it. I had an ominous feeling that the longer we remained in that damp dungeon the more likelihood there was of my losing control of events.

'I will take two of your men and trail Ana up to the gatehouse. Follow on with the others at your best speed. If any of the guards object to our departure, then so much the worse f—'

The ear-splitting crash of a discharging firearm, followed by a loud wail, cut my words short. For a few moments there was pandemonium. As the sulphurous smoke slowly cleared, a singularly unfortunate occurrence was revealed.

The guards' muskets had been distributed amongst the prisoners. In his anxiety to be ready for combat, one member of the erstwhile 'Army of the North' had reseated a percussion cap. Using far too much nervous force, he had first

116

detonated the cap with his thumb, then, in turn, the musket. The heavy ball had punched into the inner thigh of one of his compatriots. That unfortunate man had collapsed to the ground in bloody agony, whilst the perpetrator suddenly found himself with an extremely painful blister.

The whole business was in danger of degenerating into a shambles. A cursory examination revealed that the ball had miraculously missed the great thighbone, having merely ploughed a messy furrow through the man's flesh.

'A pox on the man!' I exclaimed. 'This is all we need.' Espying Ana on the stairs, I called out, 'Any undergarments that you can spare will be of use here.'

Understanding registered on her face and as I moved towards her she turned away to rummage under a voluminous skirt. Aware that most of the men were now gazing at her rather than at the wounded individual I shouldered my way through them and impatiently reached out to her. As I did so a voice called out:

'Officers only, eh? Haw-haw.'

As she handed me the material I said, 'I would be grateful if you would lead some of us back to the gatehouse. We may need your persuasive talents again. Those guards will not be eager for us to leave before they've had sight of their sergeant.'

I handed the makeshift bandaging to the nearest man, nodding an implicit instruction to make use of it.

'McCullough, Rogers,' I called out then, 'you're with me. Captain Lee, follow on with Kirby and the others. Quick as you can.'

'We will make all haste, sir.'

Satisfied, I turned away. I had deliberately not included either Buckner or Seward in my party. They had proved to be too impulsive for my tastes. I cocked my Colt Walker and carefully followed Ana up the flight of slimy steps. Behind me came the two similarly armed rangers.

On our reaching the next level I motioned for everyone to stay still. In the flickering lamplight all seemed ominously quiet. As before, the corridor was deserted. Our good fortune seemed almost improbable. As I caught Ana's eye I shrugged my shoulders and motioned for her to continue.

Up we crept, to ground level and the gatehouse beyond. Without affording me the chance to survey the scene Ana stepped boldly out into the courtyard. The sky was still dark and I had no idea how long we had until dawn. The rest of us stepped out behind her, ensuring that we kept our distance, as any respectful escort should. I had reluctantly tucked the heavy revolver into the belt behind my back. I well knew that we might have to dispatch the three fellows at the gate, but there was little point in pre-empting matters.

As it turned out, our earlier brutal conduct in the dungeon caught up with us. As Ana came before them one of the artillerymen fixed his eyes on her face, as you would upon any beautiful woman. His companions, however, seemed strangely distracted. They stared hard at her skirt, as though trying to deduce some hidden message.

My mind turned somersaults.

'Hell's teeth! What have they found?'

I didn't have long to wait.

'*Mucho sangre, señora! Por qué? Como?*'

As she struggled to make a reply they took in our presence and began to finger their muskets. McCullough hissed out one word of explanation:

'*Blood!*'

Belatedly, my mind solved the riddle. Ana had been standing very close to the sergeant when he came to a bloody end. So even in death he had given us away. This time no amounts of soft talk and fluttering eyelashes were going to disarm the *soldados*.

'Take them,' I bellowed.

As the two Texas Rangers swept up level with me I dragged the heavy weapon from behind my back. Two of the guards desperately attempted to cock and level their muskets. Such weapons are never as easy to manoeuvre as a belt gun. As the gaping muzzles of our revolvers lined up on them they must have experienced the dread that only condemned men can feel.

Both rangers fired at once. The reports were deafening. Acrid smoke blanketed us. High-pitched screaming echoed round the courtyard and for a tortured moment I thought that Ana must have taken a ball.

A rapid advance into clear air showed the true picture. My men had performed well. One Mexican lay with his skull effectively destroyed by a heavy-calibre ball. Blood and brain matter had splashed everywhere. The other unfortunate had been hit in the groin. He was slumped forward on his knees, emitting a shrill keening sound. But what of the third man?

He had been altogether more cunning. Realizing his disadvantage, he had simply discarded his musket. He had seized Ana, drawn his seventeen-inch-socket bayonet and positioned its point on her delectable neck. He applied just enough pressure to draw blood, leaving us in no doubt as to his intent. One shove and she would be skewered. Sheer terror spread over Ana's face as she realized her predicament. All three of us stopped in our tracks.

The guard had the wit to state his demand with one recognizable English word. '*Pistolas* . . . down.'

I could feel the eyes of my companions boring into me. I knew exactly what they were thinking: *WHAT'S SHE TO US? LET HIM KILL THE BITCH, THEN WE'LL FINISH HIM!*

From various sectors of the fortress came cries of alarm. The gunfire had well and truly stirred up the dons.

'*Pistolas* . . . down,' came the repeated demand.

119

Even in the poor light I could see that our opponent was sweating profusely. Yet I didn't doubt that he would carry out his implied threat. His features held the look of a man brutalized by his profession. Yet I had to do something. If we remained at an impasse he had won, because we would be swept up by his emerging *compadres.*

'Lower your weapons,' I commanded. Glancing to my left, I observed expressions of total disbelief. 'Now,' I hissed.

Ever so reluctantly the rangers lowered their revolvers. As I followed suit the swarthy Mexican allowed himself a triumphant smirk. The cries of his fellow guards were getting closer. As Ana trembled in his grip he turned slightly to summon them. My revolver was still cocked. I had one chance only.

I swept the heavy weapon up to shoulder height and rapidly sighted down the nine-inch barrel. The sudden movement registered in the man's peripheral vision. As his head turned I squeezed the trigger. With a roar the piece bucked in my hand. The heavy ball struck him in the lower jaw, shattering bone and teeth. Its momentum threw him backwards carrying Ana with him to the ground. Mercifully, the bayonet fell from his lifeless fingers. With her face now streaked with blood and brain matter Ana lay on top of her captor, too stunned to move.

Unfazed by the turn of events, McCullough just couldn't resist a ribald comment.

'That Dutch gal falls for any man she sees!'

Rogers swiftly added: 'That was mighty fine shooting, only them fellas ain't gonna like it none.'

In support of that assertion came a shouted challenge. I bounded forward to reach Ana's recumbent form. I dragged her none too gently to her feet and propelled her towards the gatehouse. Unless it contained 'murder holes', we would at least have shelter from above.

From somewhere behind us a musket discharged. The ball slammed into stone near my head before ricocheting harmlessly off into the night. I dropped into a crouch and was joined by Rogers and McCullough.

'Have a care whom you shoot at,' I reminded them. 'The others can't be far behind.'

More shots rang out, resulting in balls striking the earth and stone around us. The prison barracks had obviously contained a fair few soldiers, making it certain that our position would soon become untenable. The two rangers fired back at the muzzle flashes and there came a scream of pain. Such tactics worked both ways, however, and it could only be a matter of time before one of us was hit. The exchange of fire had brought Ana back to her senses.

'*Tu loco*,' she screamed at me. 'You could have shot *me*!'

'Better that,' I replied, 'than to be skewered by a rusty bayonet. Besides, if we don't get help soon it won't matter.'

The Lord above must have heard me, because at that moment there came a fusillade of shots. Only this time I recognized the unmistakable crash of Samuel Colt's revolver. Lee, Kirby and the others spread out across the courtyard, firing rapidly. Muzzle flashes burst forth in the dark. Cries of anguish and dismay filled the night and all resistance swiftly melted away. The fortress guards had been assigned to supervise a motley assortment of prisoners under lock and key, not to fight a pitched battle with well-armed rangers.

Elation welled up within me as I realized that we had pulled it off. Once across that causeway we could disappear into the night, where Davey and the horses awaited us. The new additions to our forces would have to ride double, but the odds on our getting clear would still be good.

Sergeant Kirby trotted towards me, sporting a broad grin.

'We sure settled them fellas. Reckon you be right glad to see us.'

121

'You did, and I am, Sergeant. But we've no time to waste. All that gunfire will have alerted the garrison. Instruct the men to pick up any muskets and cartridge boxes. We leave immediately.'

Barely had the men accomplished my bidding when there came the sound of many marching feet. I stepped out on to the causeway and gazed across it at the town of Perote. Moving out from the vague mass of buildings was a large body of men in a column of fours.

Even the usually composed Virginian appeared non-plussed.

'How can this be? No such troop formation could be mobilized that quickly.'

For one recently freed Texan the situation was all too clear.

'All is lost,' he stated despairingly.

'Like hell it is!' I blurted out. 'Sergeant, get those gates shut. Mr Lee, detail some men to lock the guards up. I'm going on to the walls.'

Peering down on the rutted stretch of road I watched as the Mexican force cleared the town. Behind the infantry came a train of artillery. Somehow their commander had foreseen a need for such weapons. Again, how could that be?

The answer to the enigma arrived on a white steed. The splendid horse could not have been his, but there was no doubting that His Excellency General Lopez de Santa Anna had just arrived on the scene.

CHAPTER NINE

'The goddamned cockchafer,' snarled Kirby. 'You know what this means, don't you? If he's prancing and preening over yonder, then Davey's kilt for sure.' He unslung his rifle, leaned on the parapet and took careful aim. 'He's had this coming for years.'

The sudden appearance of Ana's father also meant that we had most likely lost all our horses, some of our powder and ball and any element of surprise. In addition, General Ampudia presumably knew exactly what we were about. The only crumb of solace was that Santa Anna was now exactly where the President of the United States wanted him to be.

With great reluctance I placed my hand tightly over the hammer, so preventing Kirby from retracting it.

'You know I can't let you do that, Sergeant.'

'Like hell you can't! That 'tarnal bastard's kilt one of my boys *and* sold us out.'

'If you kill him, *all* the lives lost will have been for nothing,' I replied with genuine regret. 'Jack gave us a job to do and we've done it. Don't throw it all away.'

Ignoring the activity around us as our men lined the walls, Kirby fixed his cold eyes on mine. He stared long and hard. Such attention had dissuaded many a man from his chosen path, but I was not for turning. Finally the ranger emitted a great sigh. 'Well at least let me kill his poxy horse. Shake him up some.'

'I need your word that that's all you'll do.'

'Oh man! You'd squeeze a fella until the pips spewed out.'

I said nothing more. I just stood there with my hand firmly clamped over the hammer.

'All right. God damn it, yes! My word on it.'

Smiling grimly, I removed my hand. As I glanced around I could see that we had become the centre of attention. The sergeant settled himself on the rough stone and cocked his piece.

'Hold fire, boys,' he called out. 'This one's for Davey.'

The newcomers merely shrugged uncomprehendingly; even a couple of our rangers, slower-witted than the rest, failed to understand the significance of Santa Anna's presence beyond the walls. Before my attention returned to Kirby's target, I happened to notice that one of the released men was in earnest discussion with Lee. It stayed in my mind; that officer was not one to indulge in idle chitchat with the 'other ranks'.

As though nature was in furtive collusion with us, the first light of dawn announced itself. Santa Anna, mindful of the rangers' prodigious accuracy, was taking care to use the column as a shield. For some reason he was gesticulating wildly at the artillery. Possibly they weren't advancing swiftly enough, or just maybe someone's tunic was undone. Such trivia would soon be forgotten, because the general was about to receive a most unwelcome surprise.

Ranger Sergeant Kirby, serving with the First Texas Mounted for the duration of the war, was a master of his craft. His knowledge of windage and elevation came as second nature. I estimated the distance at less than two hundred yards and therefore no great challenge with a rifle. Yet poor light and many obstructions combined to make it an awkward shot. Silently levelling his weapon, he sighted down the long barrel. He allowed himself the luxury of time, taking several deep breaths to steady himself. I half-expected him to spew out a stream of tobacco juice, but then recalled that he had temporarily sworn off the weed. It had been giving him heartburn.

With a sharp crack the powder charge detonated, the explosion propelling the ball to its destination. Even as his shoulder absorbed the recoil Kirby knew that his aim had been true. A huge cheer went up along our line as Santa Anna's magnificent white horse reared up in mortal shock. The men naturally assumed that the great man himself had been struck, but I knew differently. As blood poured from its side the stricken beast settled back on its haunches before finally collapsing to the ground.

Its rider just managed to throw himself clear, falling heavily in the process. As various flunkeys rushed to help the former president to his feet I patted Kirby on the shoulder, then turned away. An unwelcome surprise awaited me. Standing directly behind us was His Excellency's rebellious daughter. Her features were ashen, yet strangely she had made no effort to disrupt the proceedings.

Our eyes met and I attempted a conciliatory smile.

'I regret that you had to witness that,' I told her. 'Believe me when I say that, but for me, he would now be dead rather than just badly shaken.'

She continued to regard me without saying a word. I was conscious of having many duties to attend to, but just could not break the contact. At last she spoke, yet so softly that I had to strain to hear her.

'I understand your hatred for him. He has done many bad things.'

I regarded her quizzically. 'If you should wish to rejoin him, I'm sure it can be arranged,' I stated. To my great surprise, she

125

shook her head emphatically.

'A husband whom I do not love awaits me in Mexico City.' There was that gorgeously breathy pronunciation of '*Me-hi-co*', which always set my pulse racing. As if that wasn't enough, her next remark was certainly sufficient to guarantee such a reaction.

'I believe I will return to Veracruz with you.'

Her delivery was remarkably casual. It suggested that her decision had been made on the spur of the moment.

I could feel my mouth going dry again. I had most assuredly not expected that response. Struggling to form an answer, I was rescued by a fusillade of musketry from beyond the moat. As fragments of blasted stone fell around me I hurriedly ushered her off the parapet.

'Stay below with those who haven't yet found a weapon,' I told her. As she scurried away, I called down to Lee. 'I need every man with a gun up on these walls, Captain.'

Without waiting for an acknowledgement I turned back to view the opposing forces. If there had been any doubt as to whether the Mexican troops would attack their own stronghold, then Kirby's well-placed ball had settled all that. The infantry, amounting to some two hundred, had formed up in two ranks. Whoever was in command knew his business. He had placed them some fifty yards away and their intentions were plain. A rapid and, at that range, reasonably accurate volley fire had just opened up.

This had the effect of suppressing our own fire whilst showering us with unwelcome chippings from the parapet. With a wide moat surrounding our position, advancing on a broad front would be fraught with difficulties. Scaling ladders and a tolerance of high casualties would be needed. However, once their artillery was in position the gates would be turned to matchwood and our brief tenure of the San Carlos Fortress would be over.

To merely crouch there, taking the punishment was not my way.

'Anyone with a musket, return fire,' I bellowed down the line. 'Those with rifles, try to pick off the gunners.'

Because of our position relative to the town my men were all on one section of wall, to the right of the gatehouse. Any other displacement would have meant that we were spread far too thinly. Desperate to avoid recapture, the freed prisoners worked their weapons with gusto. The ramparts were soon enveloped in sulphurous smoke.

Yet, to my trained eye, I could see that it was not enough. The Mexican numbers were sufficient to overwhelm our response. The occasional artilleryman crumpled to the ground, twitching in his death throes, but the cannon were remorselessly manoeuvred into position at the far end of the causeway. Soon there were six gaping muzzles pointing directly at our gates. The huge solid timbers suddenly seemed so very vulnerable.

From beyond the enemy's ranks there came a shrill bugle call. All firing ceased immediately. The early-morning light was now sufficiently bright for me easily to spot the officer bearing a white flag as he spurred his horse forward. I knew exactly what was coming. We were in an impossible position, so there would be no terms on offer. So it proved.

A splendidly attired young staff officer trotted along the causeway, then halted below and to the left of my position. His message was short and utterly lacking in embellishment.

'*Entregar*!' To avoid any misunderstanding he repeated it in heavily accented English. 'Surrender!'

A devilish dilemma now confronted me. If I simply surrendered we would all end up in irons, or even before a firing squad. 'His Excellency' was unlikely to intercede on our behalf. He was at last exactly where he wanted to be and had nothing to gain by repaying a debt of gratitude to me. Yet the

127

unacceptable alternative was to fight to the death.

An idea of sorts came to me, but it smacked of desperation. Possibly, if I managed to persuade our besiegers of our determination to pursue the latter course, I might just be able to extract better terms. It had to be worth a try, but as a plan it was very thin.

I was on the point of replying in that fashion when my right arm was suddenly gripped hard. Startled, I turned to find Captain Lee at my side.

'Your pardon, Major. I would speak with you as a matter of urgency.'

The tone of his voice and his facial expression confirmed that he was in deadly earnest. I nodded gravely.,

'Very well then,' I responded, 'you shall.' I leaned over the parapet and called down to the waiting flag-bearer: 'I must discuss your demand with my officers. You would oblige me by waiting. Do you understand?'

The swarthy individual below understood all right. He favoured me with a superior smile as he again uttered one word:

'*Entiendo.*'

I pulled back and motioned Lee over to the edge of the walkway.

'Right then, Captain. Out with it.'

'One of the released Texicans came to me with some intelligence. During their captivity they commenced to cut through the stonework in the rear of their cell. They laboured for some months and are well advanced. I have inspected their work. It is my belief that with renewed effort they – we – can soon be through.'

I felt as though I had been pole-axed. Such a development was totally unexpected. As I struggled to take it in I was assailed by doubts and my spirits plummeted.

'Are they deranged? For God's sake man, it's two levels down!'

'One,' he corrected sharply. 'You have forgotten the moat, sir. Which, thanks to the chalky soil, is empty. Once through the stonework, we tunnel up to the surface. With luck, the going will be easy, especially when we get close.'

'Luck!' I exclaimed. 'We'll need more than that.'

'We have got more than that, Major. You forget. I am an officer of engineers. This is what I do.'

In spite of the bleakness of our situation I chuckled. The man just seemed so sure of himself. But what he said next wiped the smile from my face.

'For your part, you must ensure that we are not discovered when we emerge, otherwise all is lost. You will need to keep their attention on the front of the fortress at all times, sir.'

'I believe I have a way to achieve that,' I replied, matching his now sombre demeanour. 'Very well then, Captain. Let's be about it. Please proceed with your plan.'

His full moustache twitched as though it had a life of its own. His obvious enthusiasm for the task took over.

'It is already under way, sir. I discovered a supply of hammers and entrenching tools. All those men who are unarmed are now working.'

Before I could comment, Kirby interrupted:

'That puffed-up soldier boy's gettin' restless, Major.'

With a sigh I gripped Lee's shoulder.

'Very well done, Captain. As you were.'

That officer's penetrating glance remained on me briefly before he nodded his acknowledgement and returned to his duty.

I turned away, unslung my shotgun and carefully retracted both hammers. The bulky weapon suddenly seemed unbearably heavy. The sergeant regarded me quizzically.

'Just what are you at?'

I ignored him and walked slowly back to the crenellated wall. Keeping the 'two-shoot' gun out of sight, I peered over.

The gaudily dressed young officer was indeed getting impatient. He shrugged theatrically when he caught sight of me. With genuine regret I heaved the big gun into the nearest embrasure and pointed it directly down at him. His attitude of studied arrogance was replaced by one of gut-wrenching horror. The silence around me seemed complete as every man caught his breath.

Gripping the forestock tightly, I squeezed both triggers. With an ear-splitting roar both barrels discharged their deadly load. The recoil battered my shoulder as the gun jerked both back and up. Dense smoke temporarily obscured my view. All I could hear was the sound of shod hoofs on the causeway's planking. The ridiculous thought came to me that I must have missed him.

Then, as the smoke cleared, I saw the true picture. The young man, barely in his twenties, lay spread-eagled before me. Even though he wore a red tunic there was no disguising the utter destruction of his torso. Blood had splashed up over his face, which still held a look of terror. Poignantly, the white flag of truce lay next to him, only now it was spattered red.

From beyond the moat came a collective roar of anger. I had most definitely attracted their full attention. Figures scurried around like overactive ants. There could be no doubt that retribution would be swift. I turned to face my own men and observed that even the hard-bitten ranger sergeant was shocked by my action.

'Land sakes, man! That youngster was only here to parlee. If that don't stir up a blue norther, nothing will.'

As usual I only grasped the general drift of his remarks, but that was enough. Closing in on him, I responded forcefully.

'Captain Lee is, this very minute, engaged in tunnelling through the rear wall. The Mexican forces *must* be kept away from there.' I gestured over the parapet. 'After this they should come at us like a bull at a gate. Once that gate is

130

breached we need to engage them in here and make them bleed. If they press hard we will make a fighting withdrawal down into the dungeon.

'So let's have your men off these walls. They serve no good purpose by being here. I want them arrayed over the court-yard, but not in line with the causeway.'

Kirby stared at me, goggle-eyed.

'You certainly know how to soldier, don't you.'

'Thank you, Sergeant. I'll take that as a compliment.'

'Take it any way you damn well please, only don't get us all kilt!'

The expected cannonade was short but highly effective. The first volley of roundshot smashed into the solid timber gates, effectively reducing them to kindling. Jagged splinters show-ered over the gatehouse. We few defenders, numbering roughly a score, were split into two groups, stationed in the courtyard on either side of the gatehouse. Consequently the spent shot was coming to rest behind and between us.

A second salvo erupted, serving to demolish whatever remained of the gates. The cannon, like most of Mexico's weaponry, were remnants of the Napoleonic wars, purchased from Great Britain. Old they may have been, but they were still brutally destructive. Lumps of masonry from the gate-house fell near us, demonstrating that even ricochets possessed tremendous power.

All of us had experience of being under fire and so remained lying flat, presenting as small a target as possible. As the dust settled a silence fell over the fortress. None of us had been hit, but the entrance was now accessible to all.

Spitting out an acrid mixture of phlegm and grit, I scram-bled to my feet and ran for the battered gatehouse. Our besiegers had two courses of action open to them and I needed to know which they would choose. If Santa Anna had

131

recovered from his brutal tumble and was in tactical command he would doubtless order an immediate bayonet charge. The lives of common soldiers had never been of any consequence to him. Conversely, if a more prudent officer were in charge, then I would expect him to offer us a 'whiff of grape'.

I peered cautiously round the gatehouse wall and found the answer that I sought. The gates having been totally obliterated, I had a perfect view across the causeway. The sweating artillerymen were busily serving their guns, six to a piece. Spongemen swabbed out the barrels. Then bags of black powder, followed by closed cylindrical tins, were being offered up to the muzzles. I had experienced canister shot before. Each container was filled with scores of musket balls. The controlled explosion disintegrated the cylinder, thereby unleashing a lethal horror amongst the opposing troops.

Each bombardier was blowing on his 'slow' match, which meant that I had little time. Once the 'ventsmen' had inserted a quick match into the vent of each gun, all would be ready. Swiftly I retraced my steps and bellowed out one word:

'Canister!'

Then I dropped to the ground.

Everyone knew what that word portended, yet if we had retired to a place of complete safety we would have been unable to return to defend our positions swiftly enough. I had no doubt that the massed infantry would sweep in as soon as the guns fell silent. I pressed my nose into the dirt and curled my arms around my head. Better a broken arm than a shattered skull!

Almost as one the guns discharged with a deafening crash and hell burst amongst us. The sound of hundreds of iron balls erupting into the courtyard and then rebounding again and again was beyond comprehension. This was rapidly followed by screams both of pain and of excitement. The cries of excitement were coming from beyond the walls, whilst the howls of pain were almost enveloping me.

Despite all the mayhem around me, I knew exactly what the approaching frenzy presaged. The Mexican infantry were in close support. However many dead and wounded we had, they would just have to wait. We were about to fight for our very survival.

I stretched myself flat out in the direction of the gate-house, levelled my reloaded shotgun and retracted both hammers. Such a weapon was ideal for the coming onslaught. Directly across from me Kirby was lining up a Colt Walker, his long iron by his side. He winked at me grimly but said nothing. We both knew what was coming.

On the causeway the tramp of many heavy boots competed with frenzied yelling as the infantry drew closer. Our not being able to see them only added to the tension. Then, like a cork exploding from a bottle, they were on us. A line of bayonets, eight abreast and roughly chest high, surged into the courtyard.

Aiming at their centre, I squeezed the first trigger. Around the yard numerous revolvers discharged in a ragged volley. Heavy smoke concealed the carnage but could not hide the screams. As it drifted slightly I saw the second rank press forward over their fallen comrades. Tensing my shoulder against the heavy recoil, I emptied the second barrel into them. My scattered companions did the same, with the result that the gatehouse passageway became choked with dead and dying men.

Remaining prone, I drew my own Colt Walker and Kirby and I sent a third volley into the blood-soaked mass. It was too much to be endured, even for regular troops. Their advance ground to a halt as those in the rear ranks comprehended that something terrible had taken place and ceased their forward motion. Their splendid blue-and-scarlet uniforms

133

were now spattered with blood and other grisly matter. Those still standing had not even had the chance to discharge their muskets. Yet, although beaten, they retired, reluctantly and in good order.

The soundness of my tactics had thus been demonstrated. By hugging the ground and seeking to defend the courtyard rather than the walls I had ensured that all our firepower was directed against our enemy's unavoidably narrow front. With their superiority in numbers negated, we could hold off any number of bayonet charges. Unfortunately, they were unlikely to indulge us with any such opportunities.

Echoing my thoughts, Kirby bellowed across:

'Reckon they won't try that again.'

'I know,' I replied. 'But we can't stay here. It'll be scaling ladders next and possibly more canister shot.'

'So where now, Major?' Kirby must have been impressed with my grasp of the situation, because he was rarely that deferential.

'Search the dead for powder, ball and caps. Theirs and ours. Take anything that could end a life. Then get everybody below. The wounded in the dungeon, the rest in the first corridor.' I thrust my shotgun at him and continued: 'Assign someone to reload this. We're going to need it again soon.'

Leaving my men to their allotted tasks, I returned with all haste to the parapet.

I squatted down before the nearest embrasure and took in the vista before me. The artillery pieces were inactive and appeared likely to remain so. That fact alone appeared to confirm that Santa Anna was not in tactical command. Had he been so, then doubtless the courtyard would have received fresh bursts of canister without any consideration being given for the wounded. As it was, I noticed a goodly number of men scurrying back to the town. I would have placed a sizeable wager that they had been detailed to return

134

with ladders. So we had bought our tunnellers a little time, after all.

As I had posted lookouts at the top of the stairs, I now proceeded down to the dungeon. My purpose was twofold. I needed to acquaint myself with the excavations and discover the extent of our casualties.

Captain Robert E. Lee was in his element. I had never seen him so animated. The dank, gloomy surroundings of the large cell affected him not one jot. He was simply bubbling with enthusiasm and was keen to share it. Oil lamps had been placed around the excavations, enabling me to see his detachment's progress quite clearly. Three large blocks of stone had been removed, creating an opening large enough for a man to crawl through. How much of that could be credited to the prisoners I was unable to deduce. What was obvious, from the torrent of cursing and blasphemy that emanated from it, was that the tunnel behind it now contained a man completely hidden from view.

'As you will observe sir, the diggings are well advanced. I have seized planking from the cots in the barracks. We do not have the luxury of time to board the floor, but there are side trees and caps for the roof to prevent collapse. The angle is steeper that I would like, but it will serve.'

'Who is in there?' I enquired.

'Seward, sir. I am using our own rangers rather than the freed men. They are much reduced.'

I was greatly impressed and said as much.

'You appear to have thought of everything, Captain. But there is one thing I would know. How long before you reach the surface?'

'One hour, possibly less. The distance is not vast, but the absence of clay means that we cannot avoid boarding out.'

135

Next I checked on the wounded. The canister shot had killed one man outright and seriously wounded two others. One had a shattered jaw, whilst the other had a ball embedded deep in his back. How would they fair during our flight from the fortress?

'Major,' bellowed one of the men from the level above. 'Them devils are on the move in the courtyard.'

CHAPTER TEN

'They came in over the walls,' bellowed Lance Buckner. 'Hordes of the cockchafers. Kirby popped a cap on 'em, but it mayn't hold them for long.'

I brushed past him and ascended the second set of uneven stone flags, coming up behind the sergeant. Without turning, he remarked softly:

'They knows where we ain't, but they ain't sure where we's at.'

I offered a restrained snort at that tortuous description. It would have been worth retaking the colonies just to improve their grasp of the English language.

'Right,' I said, thinking rapidly. 'We'll pull back and let them come looking. Get all your men down to the cells. You wait for me at the top of the stairs. Numbers don't matter any more. Buckner, you stay with me.'

That dissolute individual regarded me with some curiosity, but made no comment. As the rest of the men departed a strange silence settled on the corridor. We were in a form of limbo land, with many men both above and below us. I gestured for Buckner to cross over to the other side so that we were straddling the entrance to the stairway leading up to the courtyard.

No Mexicans had yet appeared so I took the opportunity to

recharge the empty chamber in my Colt Walker. Pour in the black powder, ram down the oversize ball, then place and lightly squeeze a percussion cap. The whole routine was like second nature to me.

The very moment that I finished, voices sounded at the top of the stairs. Bursts of rapid Spanish floated down to me. I didn't need to be a linguist to know what was afoot. An officer required his men to descend the stairs and, not surprisingly, they were reluctant. Heavy boots thumped briefly on the steps, then stopped to allow more discussion. Under cover of the heated argument Buckner and I cocked our revolvers.

From the courtyard came an emphatic snarl of command, which seemed to silence any further dispute. The boots resumed their descent. The stairway could just accommodate two abreast, so as to allow for the manhandling of prisoners to and fro. I had no intention of presenting myself before two deadly Brown Bess muskets.

I nodded sharply at Buckner, swung my left arm up and around the corner and squeezed the trigger. The deafening crash of two firearms resounded around the corridor. Pain lanced into my eardrums. Still without aiming we fired twice more up into the stairway. With a tremendous thump a blue-coated figure landed at our feet. Bizarrely he still clutched his weapon, yet appeared incapable of any movement. From above us there came an agonized wailing, which showed no signs of abating. A thick cloud of sulphurous smoke hung in the stairwell, hiding us from view. Taking comfort from its opacity, my companion drew his knife and leaned forward.

As the wounded soldier recognized his awful predicament his features contorted into a terrified grimace. Apparently incapable of speech, it was left to his saucer-like eyes to plead for mercy. Yet it wasn't pity that prompted me to call out to the ranger. Smoke, as protection, is merely an illusion and in no way proof against powder and ball.

Ignoring me, Buckner knelt down next to the supine Mexican and sliced his blade deep into the man's neck. As blood welled up over the metal, he smiled contentedly. It proved to be the last thing he ever did.

A volley of shots rang out above us and his head disintegrated like a ripe melon. Brain matter spattered over my trousers. Angered by his unnecessary death, I fired twice more up the stairway, prompting further spasms of pain in my ears.

My return fire dissuaded the Mexicans from advancing again, but I knew what their next move would be. With the fresh smoke concealing my retreat, I backed off to the stairs. I darted across the corridor and dropped down next to Kirby. He eyed me speculatively.

'You know how many dead we got now?'

'Nine, excluding Tylee.'

'You counted, huh?'

Our eyes locked briefly and he favoured me with a slight smile before adding softly: 'Anyhow, Rance always was a chowderhead. So, what's their next move gonna be?'

'You're asking me?'

'Why not? You're kind of a useful soldier – and our officer!'

'Very well,' I replied. 'They'll most likely drop something very unpleasant down those stairs to clear the corridor and then come in a rush. If it's an explosive round we might have an opportunity.'

Kirby was openly puzzled. 'Why so?'

'Because if they don't trim the fuse to the correct length I might have an opening.'

The sergeant was aghast. 'You're wrong in the head. Get it off beam and you're blown all to hell!'

Crouched together on the stairs as we were, his rancid breath was almost as dangerous. From the courtyard there came a shouted command.

'*Ahora mismo!*'

Almost immediately a tremendous clatter resounded on the stone flags. A very heavy object was on its way down to the passageway. Jumping to my feet, I drew my knife and raced to meet it. It was pure lunacy really, but in the heat of the moment I suspended all thought and just ran.

As the circular object crashed into view, I heard an insistent hissing noise. It came to rest next to the two bloodied cadavers. Smoke rose up towards me as I reached down to grab the fuse. There was barely one inch remaining as I sliced through it. I tossed it away from me and stepped sharply back to the wall on the left of the stairwell. I unslung my shotgun, eased back both hammers and waited. As before, silence descended on the corridor. This time I was alone, save for two corpses and an inert cast-iron explosive shell. If the gunner had done his work properly, I should by then have consisted solely of unrecognizable lumps of bloodied meat and bone.

From above there came the sound of angry recriminations. I could well imagine their frustration. They had observed the fuse bursting into life, so there was no logical reason for its failure. What there was, however, was an understandable reluctance to investigate. Many minutes passed before anyone could be intimidated into action; such delay was just what I was striving for.

Eventually there came the sound of movement around the entrance. This time I did not expect anyone to fully descend the stairs. All I needed was a normal level of human curiosity and a certain obedience to authority. I was not to be disappointed. The natural light of morning suddenly decreased, blocked out by a human form. At the same time there was a gentle scuffle, as someone tentatively eased on to a stone step. That was accompanied by whispering, as some no doubt browbeaten junior officer encouraged the unfortunate individual to proceed. I pushed away from the wall, aimed my

140

shotgun up towards the sounds of this activity and squeezed the triggers.

Both powder chambers detonated with a tremendous crash. Simultaneously I felt a sharp jolting pain in my right ear. I staggered back, convinced that somehow I had been shot. Then I sensed some form of liquid trickling down my right cheek and I knew exactly what had happened. My much-abused right eardrum had finally burst.

From above there came more screaming. The men up there had been badly used. Retaliation was bound to be swift. There was absolutely no chance that they would allow me to repeat my trick. Feeling nauseated and greatly unsettled, I stumbled back to rejoin Kirby. Genuine concern clouded his grizzled features.

'You don't look too good, Thomas.'

His words sounded strangely distant, as though we were sharing a dream. Just managing to summon a faint smile, I responded:

'Neither of us will if we don't get out of here.'

Then I felt the bile rise in my throat and I twisted away from him. Vomit spewed forth on to the already greasy stone flags. I just needed to sit still and collect myself but Kirby wasn't having any of it. He reached under my armpits and heaved me to my feet. But for his firm grasp I would have slipped on my own mess. Together we weaved our way unsteadily down to the dungeon.

On reaching the outer chamber I spied Ranger Seward, dirty and dishevelled after his tunnelling stint. He opened his mouth to pass some comment but we never did benefit from his wisdom. From above came a tremendous explosion that seemed to shake the very walls. Dust and mortar showered down on us, yet before we had time to react there was another detonation of similar magnitude.

Still dazed from my injury I turned back to the stairs,

valiantly clutching my empty shotgun. The sergeant's iron grip descended on my right arm, bringing me to an abrupt halt.

'Whoa there. They'll be right behind them shells and you're no good to us dead. We need you.' Guiding me gently towards the cell he continued: 'Besides, your big gun ain't even loaded. Seward, follow us in and lock the door. Might slow them down some.'

As my senses returned I realized that there was logic to his thinking. It was highly likely that two more explosive shells would come tumbling down those stairs. The Mexicans had learnt their lessons the hard way.

Gratefully I dropped down near the diggings, then noticed Ana sitting alone in the far corner of the large cell. Captain Lee displayed genuine concern at my appearance.

'You appear somewhat reduced, Major. What ails you?'

'Pray do not trouble yourself, Captain. It is merely a burst eardrum. I shall live.' Struggling to marshal my thoughts, I continued: 'How goes the tunnel? I fear that we shall be hard pressed shortly.'

Behind him I could see one of Kirby's few remaining rangers scooping fresh earth out of the tunnel's mouth.

'We will be through in the merest hint of time, sir,' replied the engineer confidently. His blue uniform was showing signs of wear and tear but its wearer was clearly in his element. 'Might I suggest that you stay well clear of the door? Splinter wounds can be most grievous.'

Seward, having just turned the heavy key in the lock, grimaced and backed away fast. Yet we were not to be assaulted quite so soon. A familiar voice boomed out from the top of the stairs.

'Major Collins, I would speak with you, *por favour*.'

Santa Anna!

'What on earth can that man want?' My question was

142

foolish and ill-judged. Lee, knowing that I was out of sorts, refrained from comment. Not so Kirby, of course.

'She done us a service, but she's still his bitch!'

The man definitely had a pleasing way about him.

I staggered to my feet and instructed Seward to unlock the door.

'Is that wise, sir?' queried Lee.

'I'll talk, while you dig,' I replied, smiling weakly. 'We have nothing to lose, and everything to gain.'

I passed through the doorway and thrust my shotgun at Seward.

'Load this. We'll very likely need it before long.'

I cocked my Colt Walker and approached the foot of the stairs. The gun only had one chamber remaining, but it looked a damn sight more imposing than the Paterson. Hugging the wall, I called out:

'Show yourself, General. You have nothing to fear from me.'

His reply was instantaneous yet slightly muted, suggesting that he was positioned well out of sight.

'Of that I am sure, but not from your men, I think.'

'They do as they are ordered. No more, no less.'

'Fine words, Major. Fine words. But no matter.' His voice sounded louder so I moved away from the wall, but only slightly. Remaining partly concealed, I peered up the stairs. There before me stood His Excellency Antonio Lopez de Santa Anna. His magnificence was tarnished slightly by an ill-fitting tunic, stained with both blood and earth. It had indeed been a heavy landing.

'I would speak plainly, Major. I can offer you no terms. The young officer whom you so ungallantly slaughtered was General Ampudia's son.'

'That was unfortunate,' I replied. But still, I could not allow him the moral high ground. 'And what of young Davey?

He was also someone's son.'

I had hoped at least to confirm the young ranger's demise, but it was not to be. Santa Anna regarded me impassively for some moments. When eventually he spoke again it was as though I had never interrupted him.

'When we attack you, as we must, then I too will lose a child. A child for whom you appear to have a certain affection. I implore you to release her.'

I knew full well his capability for lies and deceit, but there was no denying the true emotion contained in his words. He stood with his arms outstretched before him. The artificial light was too poor for me to see his eyes, yet it would not have surprised me if they had been moist. Consequently my own reply was also honest in its own way.

'It was her own decision to come with me. Yet I cannot allow that to be the cause of her death. Permit me a moment to put this to her.'

He bowed silently, making no move to stand off. I pulled back, turned and made for the cell door. If nothing else, all this gave Captain Lee a bit more time.

My reception was not what I had expected. Kirby stood in the doorway. He was chewing tobacco manically, the proof of its nature evident when he spat out a stream on to the dirt floor. He appeared more unsettled than I had ever seen him before.

'The only way that looker leaves here without us is with her tongue cut out. Shoot! First thing she does on reaching those stairs is speak on that.' He gestured wildly towards the hole in the cell wall.

'That's lunacy,' I protested. 'It's thanks to her that we released your countrymen.'

'So tell Santa Anna to go screw himself. What happens then makes no odds. We go up the tunnel and back to Xalapa. You do with her what you will. For me, I don't reckon you've met an honest woman 'til you've found one with maggots in her eyes.'

The sheer venom contained in his words took me aback. I could only assume that in times past he had been badly used by the gentler sex.

'*Madre de Dios*! You allow this *bestia* to talk of me in such a way?'

Ana's words took me by surprise, although of course they shouldn't have. Unlike me, she did not have impaired hearing. Her eyes flared with angry reproach and, as usual when she was irate, she looked absolutely delectable.

'I cannot change how he thinks of you,' I replied. 'But you will come to no harm.' As I stated this I favoured Kirby with a warning glance. 'He is quite correct in one respect, though,' I continued, 'I can't allow you to rejoin your father just yet.'

Her expression of annoyance turned rapidly to one of hurt.

'You also think I would give away your secret?'

'What I think does not count. I have a responsibility for the lives of all these men, and you are still your father's daughter.'

With perfect timing my words were punctuated by a strongly accented voice calling from above:

'Major, I am not used to being kept waiting.'

Eyeing me expectantly, Kirby disgorged another revolting stream of dark juice.

'Escort this lady to the rear of the cell. please, Sergeant. I have business to attend to.' So saying, I pulled away and returned to the stairs.

The general regarded me with his hands on his hips, for all the world as though I were an errant schoolboy returning to the fold. If that analogy had been true, then I would shortly have been due for a sound thrashing.

'I regret that it is not possible to return Ana to you at this time.'

'For what reason?' His reply imperious.

'I have no say in the matter,' I dissembled. 'She chooses to remain of her own volition.'

Santa Anna's English was excellent but not perfect. That, together with the dubious acoustics, seemed to lead him to believe that I had actually used a variation of the word 'violate'. Consequently he began to fairly tremble with anger.

'You will release her now, unharmed, or none of you *bandidos* will see another dawn.'

My response was merely a simple shrug.

'Fair enough. Only if I were you I wouldn't send any more explosive shells our way. Not if you want to see Ana again.'

With that I turned away. His Excellency had food for thought, and Captain Lee had gained some more time.

A short while later, as I took my ease on the cell floor, Captain Lee arrived and stood before me. Like the general's, his blue uniform was somewhat dirty and dishevelled. Unlike the general, he was in fine humour.

'We have broken the surface, sir. All is quiet above. It seems that all their attention is focused inside the fortress.'

His delivery had been calm and controlled. There had been no celebratory whoops of joy from the tunnel. He had exerted iron control over his men and again I was much impressed. I clambered to my feet and took his hand.

'I am most grateful for your efforts, Captain. Do I take it that we can now leave this foul place?'

'Very shortly, sir. The final cap and side trees have to be placed, otherwise the exit could collapse in on us. There will be many of us crawling through it.'

Before I could respond I was interrupted by a loud expletive from near the cell door.

'You better see this, Major,' called Kirby. 'They're on the move.'

146

'All haste, Captain,' I urged, moving off to join the sergeant. 'We need to be gone from here.'

The sight that greeted my eyes was unexpected, yet it really shouldn't have been. The Mexicans' next ploy was an obvious tactic against men besieged underground. A thick cloud of black smoke was swiftly filling the chamber directly outside the cell door. I caught a whiff of it and recoiled at the foul odour.

'Clever, very clever,' I muttered softly.

'What in tarnation is that stuff?'

'It's a smoke ball,' I replied. 'Concentric sheets of paper filled with a mixture of powder, saltpetre, pitch, coal and tallow. I believe the British invented it.'

'You think the British invented everything,' he retorted sarcastically. 'But I'll allow it could give us pause.'

Keenly aware of the urgency, I pondered how to combat the latest threat. We could not see anything through the vile cloud, which was continuing to spread. But then again, neither could they. No one could breathe in it; therefore a steady advance on our position was impossible. Ana's presence ruled out more shells. That only left a sudden rush by as many infantry as they could cram down the stairs. A man would need to take a deep breath and hold it as he charged through the smoke.

'Get some men on this door,' I hissed.

Kirby motioned for his men to advance on him, then a thoughtful look spread over his face.

'Pull back boys. Some on either flank. Give them a bottle-neck.' He turned the heavy key in the lock, then tossed it nonchalantly into the filthy straw.

The men with us were all released prisoners, thereby leaving Kirby's rangers to act as temporary tunnellers. Although unfit and malnourished, they were keen and able to pull a trigger. They all knew that they were fighting for their lives.

147

I glanced back to ensure that Ana was out of the line of fire. She chose to feign ignorance of my attention, yet she appeared jittery and on edge. I didn't like the signs, and resolved to keep a close watch on her. But how can anybody do that when they are about to fight for their life?

From beyond the evil billowing smoke, came the sounds of many men on the move: metal on metal, involuntary coughs, the scuffle of boots and whispered commands.

'Cock your pieces, boys.' Kirby's command, although mostly superfluous, was a steadying influence.

Then, from off to my left, came Captain Lee's calm voice.

'We're ready for you, Major.'

I acknowledged his mild statement with a cursory nod, then eased back the hammers of my reloaded shotgun. His burrow would have to wait. The last thing we needed was to be caught by a line of bayonets whilst evacuating the cell.

The attack, when it came, was eerily silent. No wild screams or bellowed insults. The lack of air prevented all that. It was the pounding of many pairs of boots that announced the men's arrival in the outer chamber. A bearded face under a dark-blue, red-rimmed felt cap appeared at the open grille. Then there sounded a tremendous splintering crash as the door received a mighty blow. As Kirby discharged his revolver at the grim figure his identity came to me. General Ampudia, or whoever was in charge, had had the foresight to send in Pioneers with the first wave. Wearing sapper's aprons and carrying large axes, their role was to break a way through enemy fortifications. They had been utilized to great effect in the final assault on the Alamo.

Kirby's heavy ball smashed into a set of misshapen yellow teeth and the apparition disappeared from sight. But another and then another took his place. The sturdy door received more shattering blows before abruptly surrendering to the

148

inevitable. As it suddenly swung open, a Pioneer was flung into the cell by the momentum of his abruptly redundant stroke. Before he could recover his balance a musket ball struck his upper torso, throwing him back into his comrades.

It failed to check their progress however. They were just too blind and too desperate to get away from the choking smoke. As the closely following Mexican infantry trampled over their comrade and burst into the cell a ragged musket volley crashed out around me. Agonized screams reverberated throughout the room and beyond. Through the patchy clouds of fresh smoke I could just make out the twitching bodies sprawled around the entrance. We had hit them hard, but only on a narrow front. The bottleneck was working against both sides and they had far more men than we had.

I levelled the big gun and allowed half a dozen soldiers to crowd in before firing. Having steeled myself against the tremendous roar I found that it was actually my left ear that now pained me. Yet the scene of pure carnage before me overwhelmed any such discomfort. The assorted shot had ripped through flesh and blood, laying low any that it touched. But it still wasn't enough. The relentless pressure from behind to escape the sulphurous smoke propelled more soldiers into the cell. With Kirby's men apparently either in the tunnel or in the moat above, our defence was left to men with mostly empty weapons.

Our assailants discharged their muskets and some of the balls struck home. Then, to the accompaniment of the anguished cries of their victims, they moved in with cold steel. I defy anyone to remain calm in the face of such a visceral menace. The situation had become truly terrifying. A razor-sharp seventeen-inch blade lunged at me. Desperately deflecting it with the barrels of my shotgun, I charged forward. I got close enough to my attacker to see the tears streaming from his red-rimmed eyes.

'God's blood!' I bellowed. 'They're all half blind.'

With vicious precision, I slammed the wooden stock into his left cheekbone. As his head snapped back the uniform shako tumbled almost comically to the floor. Giving no quarter, I pounded the bridge of his nose with the gun butt. No one could withstand such cruel treatment. As the vanquished soldier fell back I rapidly turned to face a new threat.

I only just made it. Another bayonet loomed before me, only this time there was no unguarded lunge. The man behind it appeared old to be still in the ranks but he knew his trade. He approached steadily, flicking the blade from side to side, so as to prevent me flanking him. I had nowhere to go but back. Back to the wall and certain death!

There was only one course left to me. I shifted my grip on the shotgun and lobbed the heavy weapon over his guard, directly at his face. With both hands occupied he had no option other than to step sharply back. The sawn-off clattered harmlessly to the ground, but it had provided a necessary breathing space. Seizing my nearest available belt gun, I cocked the .36 Paterson Colt and aimed it directly at my assailant's torso. A misfire then would surely have finished me.

With a reassuring crash the revolver served its owner well. The ball struck the infantryman square in the chest. He tottered, as though about to fall and that should have been the end of it. Yet, amazingly, he summoned reserves of strength that first kept him vertical and then allowed him to resume his lethal advance.

Frantically I retracted the hammer and took a very deliberate two-handed aim at his face. The eyes were burning with manic determination. The approaching bayonet was as steady as a rock. I would only have the one chance. I drew in a deep breath and squeezed the trigger.

The beautiful muzzle flash confirmed my survival. The

second ball struck the grizzled veteran directly between the eyes. As his head snapped back, blood and brain matter exploded from the rear of his skull. Ignoring his now harmless presence and with three chambers remaining, I turned to confront the next challenge.

There wasn't one!

Lee, Seward and the remaining rangers had emerged from the tunnel and were unleashing a deadly repeating fire upon the remaining soldiers. For men barely able to see it was all too much. They broke and ran for their lives.

Relief flooded through me. We had done it. Somehow the majority of us had survived. I searched out Kirby.

'We should go now, before they regroup,' I hissed.

The man blinked twice, as though gathering his thoughts. He leaned back against the wall to catch his breath. There was an ugly gash on his forehead, but he seemed to be otherwise unscathed.

'You're a real push-hard, ain't you, Thomas?'

'That's why I'm a commissioned officer and you're just an enlisted man, Sergeant!' I replied, adopting the same lightly bantering tone.

Despite the gore surrounding us, a wry smile crept over his weary features.

'Can't argue with that. Besides, I'm all wore out. Getting too long in the tooth for this kind of shindig.'

Before I could respond, a figure in cream and white raced past me, heading for the outer chamber.

'Ana!' I cried.

Too late to block her way, Kirby did exactly what I would have expected of him. He pushed clear of the damp wall, then cocked and levelled his revolver. My skin crawled with shock as I cried out again:

'Ana, don't do it.'

Without turning she paused outside the cell. The choking

smoke had dissipated slightly, but the stairway was still obscured. Rather than enter the murk, she chose instead to call after her father's troops.

'*Alto, alto! Estan cavando*—'

She did not get the chance to say any more. Her strident words were cut short by two loud gunshots.

CHAPTER ELEVEN

Ana's voluptuous body was flung back like a rag doll's. One musket ball had slammed into the doorframe, only inches from Kirby's head. The other had struck Santa Anna's daughter in the throat. The ranger's weapon remained unfired, but only because the fleeing Mexicans had discharged their pieces first.

Oblivious to any remaining threat, I rushed over to her. With a heavy heart I cradled her head in my hand and gazed down at her. I had seen enough wounds in my time to know that she could not possibly survive hers. Anguish welled up inside me, as I watched the blood frothing from her mouth. As her eyes met mine, I smiled weakly and caressed her jet-black hair. She struggled to say something, but could not form the words. Close behind me, Kirby called out remorselessly:

'We need to move, Thomas.'

I shook my head in despair.

'Allow me a minute, damn you!'

Gazing down at her, I saw the light leave her eyes. As she emitted a low moan her body shivered in an uncontrollable tremor. Then a stillness settled over her as all life departed. Her head lolled sideways into my cupped hand, never to rise again. She had not deserved such a brutal and meaningless end.

I would have remained in that highly vulnerable position had not Kirby again hissed at me.

'They'll be back, Thomas. We gotta move – *now*!'

Coming to my senses, I gently lowered Ana's head to the floor. It seemed unbelievably callous just to leave her there, but there was nothing else for it. At least she would be found by her own kind. As though confirming that, there sounded much coughing in the corridor above. A lot of the sulphurous smoke had drifted up the stairs. With that and the heavy casualties to contend with, I felt confident that it would be some time before the Mexicans renewed their attack. I rejoined the others in the cell and sought out Robert Lee.

'Let's have everybody out, Captain.'

'Everybody, sir?' The engineer scrutinized me keenly.

I knew exactly what he meant, yet I had dreaded the question. We had taken a number of casualties and not all had been fatal.

'Everybody through the tunnel. Those that can walk will take their chances with us. The rest must wait in the moat. I will not leave any man down here.'

Despite the difficulties involved Lee accepted my decision without protest. He fully understood my reasoning. When the enemy infantry finally stormed the cell, they would be in an uncontrollable killing frenzy. Fierce resistance would be expected. No quarter would be given. My fervent hope was that by the time our wounded were discovered in the moat tempers might have cooled somewhat.

As the men began crawling through the narrow opening I returned to the shattered cell door. Kirby was reloading his revolver whilst watching the stairs. Without comment I pushed the battered door closed and then surveyed the scene. The room resembled a slaughterhouse. All around us lay bloodied corpses.

Espying my shotgun partly concealed amongst the bodies,

I suddenly realized that they could serve a purpose.

'Lend a hand here,' I called over to the sergeant.

Grabbing hold of arms and legs, we piled the enemy cadavers up behind the door. There seemed to be a certain justice in hindering the enemy's advance with its own men. I paused for breath and looked through the door grille. Ana's broken body lay before me, an isolated and pitiful sight.

'I don't think I ever really understood her,' I remarked sadly.

'Don't ever try,' Kirby remarked sagely. 'Women are a whole nuther thing. And that one had enough tongue for ten rows of teeth.'

Reluctantly I tore myself away from the aperture and glanced back into the room. The prison cell was empty. The last of the injured men was being eased into the tunnel. His cries of distress brought me back to the present. The bloody wound in his belly would ensure a slow and painful death. To be skewered by Mexican bayonets might actually have provided a welcome relief, but in all conscience I couldn't have left him to such a fate.

'Come,' I said to Kirby. 'We should go.'

'Help me drag these fellas over to cover the tunnel,' he replied, indicating two of the dead Americans. 'They're past caring and it might set them greasers to wondering just where we are.'

Anything that served to delay pursuit was worth trying, so together we heaved the two former prisoners over to the entrance. They were lighter than I had expected, but after months of captivity it was hardly to be wondered at. Then, as the ranking officer, I ushered Kirby into the tunnel ahead of me.

'You ain't fixing on going down with the ship are you?' he asked.

His fount of dry wit was endless. Nevertheless, the thought

155

of a doomed last stand held a certain charm when weighed against crawling into a small dark space. Reluctantly, I got on to my hands and knees and entered the tunnel.

I was immediately assailed by a strong sense of claustrophobia. Ahead and above me the light of day was visible, but the roof was low and the passage narrow. God knows how they had managed to drag the wounded men up it. I twisted round and reached out to grab hold of the nearest cadaver's leather belt. With all my strength I pulled the body towards me until it was level with the entrance. With luck, our escape route would be totally obscured from view.

The intense effort combined with the lack of fresh air had caused beads of sweat to form on my face. With one end of the tunnel now blocked off, irrational fear swept over me. The light seemed much reduced. What if there was a cave-in? What if I got jammed between the side trees?

I was saved from making a complete ass of myself by Lee's appearance at the exit. As ever, his reading of the situation was spot on.

'If this is your first time in such tight circumstances, I suggest you keep your head down and just crawl, sir.'

Which is exactly what I did. Despite the gradient, the tunnel was only a few yards long and I was up it in no time. Suddenly finding my head and shoulders in the moat was a surreal experience. All of my recent planning had gone into achieving just that, yet once there we were still in very real danger.

We had surfaced just beyond the base of the rear wall, completely out of sight of the front of the fortress. There were no guards visible on the parapet above us. Hardly surprising, as we were all supposed to be trapped in the bowels of the prison.

Our six wounded men presented a sorry sight as they lay sprawled about in varying degrees of distress. Amongst their number was the singularly unfortunate individual who had been shot in error by his own comrade. For him, fate had been especially cruel. I felt bitterly unhappy at having to leave them, but there was nothing else for it.

None of us made mention of returning to our former bivouac. Santa Anna's sudden appearance had meant that Davey was very probably dead. His Excellency was not the sort to burden himself with a prisoner. Our horses and supplies must have been seized, unless they remained there as part of an elaborate trap. Either way they were lost to us.

Glancing round at my two immediate subordinates I observed their vastly differing expressions. Captain Lee, regular career soldier, was quite obviously basking in self-satisfaction at a job well done. Sergeant Kirby, hard-bitten frontier volunteer, recognized the daunting task ahead of us.

'However you look at it,' that man commented drily, 'we got us a hell of a long walk!' Gesturing beyond the moat he continued: 'How d'you read this. One at a time, or all at a rush?'

There was no doubt in my mind.

'Whether they spot one or all of us makes no difference. We have to cover as much distance as possible.'

After casting a final glance at the forlorn wounded I urged every man standing to make for the edge of the moat. It was only then that the reality of just how few of us had survived hit home. Of the original twenty that had left Veracruz, there now remained only six of us: Lee, Kirby, myself and three rangers. Because the released prisoners had taken the brunt of the fighting in the dungeon their numbers were reduced to a round dozen.

I soon realized that running was hard work, especially when laden down with a shotgun, two revolvers and assorted ammunition. On reaching the stone wall bordering the moat I turned to view the fortress, convinced that we must be discovered.

Not a soul was in sight, either on the walls or around the grim structure. Only the broken bodies of our own comrades were visible. If we could just get out of the moat and off into the broken ground we stood a chance.

Seward and Kirby scrambled up the steep sides, then stood guard as the rest of us followed. Were we actually going to get away with it?

The worn slabs provided plenty of handholds, allowing me to clamber up with ease. The tension, however, was almost unbearable. All the time I expected to feel the massive shock of a musket ball slamming in between my shoulder blades. It never came. As I reached the edge my eyes locked briefly with those of Captain Lee. He favoured me with a warm smile, but there was no disguising the pressure that even he was feeling.

When everyone was out of the moat I issued one simple command.

'Now then, men, let us run like the devil until we are out of sight of both the prison and the town.'

After that I didn't have the breath to spare for any words of encouragement. Eighteen tired, dirty, bloodstained men ran as though the hounds of hell were after them.

Once away from the fortress we were soon on to broken ground. Rocks and stunted trees provided little cover, but a steady downhill gradient eased our task. The going was precarious, so that it was some time before I risked a backward glance. What it showed was a clear skyline. With Perote finally out of direct sight, it would take a sweep by cavalry for the Mexicans to find us. Our chances were improving by the minute.

I caught sight of Captain Robert E. Lee, still sporting Santa Anna's garish tunic. For some reason he held my attention. Calmly and professionally, he was chivvying the released prisoners into action.

'That man could just go on to greater things,' I mused.

CHAPTER TWELVE

'So, where next for you then, Thomas?'

Colonel John Coffee Hays, or Jack to his many friends, observed me closely. He was lounging on the cot situated at the rear of his tent. There was no sign of the grey pallor visible at our previous encounter. Whatever service Travis had performed in his oral cavity had obviously been successful.

'I'm leaving for the coast with the next column of sick and wounded. It appears that I'm not needed round here any more.'

His thin face creased into a strained smile. Although outwardly relaxed the colonel proved to be suffering inner turmoil. After noisily clearing his throat his speech was noticeably forced.

'Somebody has to tell you this. I kind of reckon it should be me. News has just reached us that Santa Anna has deposed President Farias and seized power.'

I responded with a caustic laugh. So far so good. His revelation had failed to surprise me, but there was more to come.

'His excellency has followed popular opinion and vowed to rid the country of all gringo invaders. As expected, he has played us false.'

As my memory of the dreadful return journey from Perote flooded back, I dropped down on to the cot next to Hays. It

159

had taken us many days and nights of tortuous evasion and travel before we had finally met up with the American forces at Xalapa.

'So,' I sighed. 'All those good men died for nought. Davey, Travis. . . .'

Hays responded swiftly. 'Don't ever think that, Thomas. I've heard what took place. But for your leadership that pestilential prison would still be full of our boys. I'll allow, though, that completing your mission successfully was never going to endear you to the local high command. General Scott prefers conquest to a negotiated settlement. Looks like he's going to get his wish. I'm just glad that you got out of that damned place in one piece!"

Slowly I got to my feet. I favoured him with a warm smile.

'Yes. Well, it would have been a hell of a place to die.'